Beth snak **and gave** **fighting all day—to touch her lips to his.**

The moment she did that, he let out a moan deep in his throat, his fingers fumbling, and a touch wasn't enough. Her mouth claimed his, tongue dipping inside to discover that he did, as expected, taste of warm salt and sea-spray, and something else that she couldn't identify, but immediately wanted more of. This was her dream, all of her dreams recently, only even better.

Books by Anna Leonard

Silhouette Nocturne

The Night Serpent #48
The Hunted #86

ANNA LEONARD

Anna Leonard is the nom d'paranormal for fantasy/horror writer Laura Anne Gilman, who grew up wondering why none of the characters in her favorite Gothic novels ever seemed to know a damn thing about ghosts, vampires, or how to run in high heels. She is delighted that the newest generation of heroines has a much better grasp on things. "Anna" lives in New York City, where either nothing or everything is paranormal….

Both can be reached via:
www.sff.net/people/lauraanne.gilman or
http://cosanostradamus.blogspot.com.

THE
HUNTED
ANNA LEONARD

Silhouette Books

nocturne™

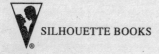

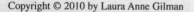

SILHOUETTE BOOKS

Recycling programs
for this product may
not exist in your area.

ISBN-13: 978-0-373-61833-0

THE HUNTED

Printed in U.S.A.

Dear Reader,

My family spent many summer vacations along the Massachusetts coast, and the sound and smell of the ocean is one of my strongest memories even now. When the idea of a selkie hero came to me, the decision to set the story on the Cape was a no-brainer. Of course, that also meant that both my hero and heroine are of the staunch Yankee breed—occasionally (often) too stubborn for their own good, but fierce when the ones they love are threatened.

Any passing resemblance to family members may not be entirely coincidental….

Laura Anne Gilman

For Amy and Larry

Prologue

Miles away, in another world, a young male in his prime leaned back, and thought about a woman.

He didn't know her name. Or what she looked like. Or the sound of her voice or her favorite foods. He didn't know anything about her, not even that she, specifically, existed. But he woke one morning to the sound of rain on the water, and couldn't stop thinking about her.

The obsession was hard on him, shadowing his every move, every hour of the day, filling his thoughts, and he didn't know what to do about it.

He rolled over on his side and stared out over the ever-moving surface of the sea. No, that wasn't the truth. He knew exactly what to do about it. He just didn't want to.

Life was good, right now. The outcropping of rock was warm underneath him, his sleek, powerful muscles slack and relaxed after a day of hard swimming, and the ocean spray tingled on his bare skin, milky-pale despite the hours spent exposed to the elements. He could stay here all day, sleep out under the cool wind and bright stars. Or he could swim back home to the little village where his family lived, the comfortable cottage where there would be fresh-caught fish on the table, and a squabble of nieces and nephews to wrestle with, and the pleasure of a new season of warmth and life to celebrate on this first full week of spring.

Life was good. On any other day, any other time of his life, he would be content with the gifts he had been given, to be alive and healthy and surrounded by everything he could possibly want.

But now something tingled in his blood, making him restless and moody. Not just this day: all week, ever since the equinox. Life might be good, but he wasn't sleeping, wasn't satisfied with the way anything tasted, wasn't taking pleasure in anything that he normally enjoyed. Even his temper, normally even and calm, was frayed and ragged.

His blood-kin abandoned him first, shaking their heads and rolling their eyes at his growls and twitches, telling him without words that they wouldn't put up with his behavior. His seal-kin lasted longer, their patient eyes and soft plush fur giving comfort until his increasing discomfort drove them away as well, searching out other places to bask in the spring sunshine and leaving him alone on the rock.

He knew what was wrong. Or rather, what was right. Even if he hadn't observed it in others, instinct would drive him. The temper, the frustration, the desire to pick a fight with his nearest and dearest... He needed to mate.

No, that wasn't accurate. He'd been through lust before, and this was...more. He needed to find the female who would stay with him, not for a night or even a season, but forever.

Somewhere out there, this woman existed. The simple fact of her being was firing his blood, making him dream of her skin, her hair, the feel of her wrapped around him, of him fitting inside her so perfectly, body and soul...

All he had to do was find her, woo her, win her.

It was a simple enough thing, in theory. Not every seal-kin partnered for life—his own mother had several mates, one of them his father, and was on good terms with them all—but it happened often enough. Always the same way: an impossible pull, tugging the male to bend to its will until the female was found and won, wooed and well mated. But the others males always seemed able to find what— who—they needed among the blood-kin, the eight Families that made up this colony. If a mate was not there, they sometimes traveled north or south, to meet up with other colonies. Places that were known, were filled with familiar names and shared histories.

He didn't feel a pull that way. He felt pulled westward. West, across the sea, toward the setting sun.

He covered his face with his arm, trying to block out the need. There were no colonies to the west that anyone knew of. Nobody had gone west in generations. He would not find what he needed.

That knowledge did not stop the pull, inexorable as the tides.

It felt wrong, to go against what was traditional. And he resented this pull his body had on him, when it wasn't what he had been planning. He hadn't even thought to take a breeding-mate for another few seasons, much less life-mating.

But his people trusted their instincts. Instinct was what kept them alive and free, even when other colonies were wiped out by Hunters, by pollution, by the slow eroding of their territories. Instinct, and not being too stubborn, too stupid to acknowledge simple truths.

So when the itch became too much, the need overwhelming, and the warmth of the rock no longer soothed, he slipped shoulder-first into the cold waters of the Atlantic, ignoring the storm clouds forming in the distant east, and, without a word of farewell to anyone, swam toward the pull.

Chapter 1

Beth Havelock was restless. She moved back and forth in her workroom, touching projects but not actually doing anything with them. The paper cutter was cleared off, the trash emptied, the work counter scrubbed, pens capped and sorted, to-file box filed down to the last proof sheet and invoice. Chemicals were sorted, the older ones pulled to the front of the darkroom's cabinet, the newer ones pushed to the back. She even changed the batteries in all the smoke detectors in the house a week early, and then, still needing something to do, went back into her workroom on the first floor and rinsed out all of the extra developing trays, setting them to dry upside down on the counter. Still, she felt the need to be moving, doing.

Her bare feet scrunched against the cold tile floor, her toes flexing and releasing as though picking up the motion her hands were forbidden, the tension thrumming through her entire body, nose to toes.

"Good lord, what *is* it with you, woman?" Her voice echoed in the tile-and-chrome workroom, startling her even though she was the one who had spoken.

She was well ahead of her deadlines—waking early and restless did wonderful things to her to-do list, even if it was making her antsy beyond belief. Business was good right now, but not good enough to keep up with her sudden surge of energy, as though she had been mainlining energy drinks and chocolate rather than her usual healthy diet. Maybe she should switch to chocolate bars and soda for a week, see what that did for her.

"All that will do is give you zits like you were fourteen again," she said, horrified by the thought. "It's spring fever like usual, that's all." It wasn't anything unusual for her, for all that it seemed more severe. She got like this every year, when the weather finally began to soften, and the days started getting longer. This winter had been a particularly rough one along the New England coast, and when they weren't getting hit with surprisingly heavy snowfall, they were being battered by seemingly nonstop nor'easters. Waves and wind were nothing new to hardy Nantucketers like the Havelocks, but after several months of overcast white skies and the never-ending howl of the wind, that first day of spring, when the skies were blue and the air mild, could rouse even the most phlegmatic of New Englander into flights of relative fancy. And while Beth Havelock was many things from practical to responsible, she wasn't phlegmatic.

She also wasn't focusing at all. That really wasn't like her. Normally, once she settled in to work she could shut out any distraction, not noticing anything except what she was doing. Today, even the sound of a bird singing outside was enough to break her concentration.

She sighed, moving away from the window and staring at the far wall. It was painted a darker white than the other walls, intentionally, to better showcase the photos mounted there. Her own work ran the gamut, from a traditionally posed wedding photo of a bride and groom, to three dolphins leaping in the surf, to a single lonely form standing on the rocks at night, like a human watchtower. She was a good photographer, although not good enough to make a living at it. Her technical skills were better than her artistic ones. But sometimes she caught just the right moment, like the photograph at the end that, no matter how many times she saw it, always caught her attention: a single harp seal, pulled up onto a shelf of rock, gazing up at her with sad eyes…and one flipper raised in what, in a human, would have been a rude gesture.

Even on bad days when everything was going to crap, that photo could always make her laugh.

Today, instead, it filled her with a strange sense of wistfulness.

Giving in to her mood, she locked up the darkroom, put away her materials and, still barefoot, left the work space on the second floor of her Victorian-era home. That was the advantage to working for herself, rather than reporting to an office. Worse pay, longer hours, but moderately better perks, including the ability to work at 4:00 a.m.—or take off at 4:00 p.m. Rather than heading downstairs to the rambling porch and the enticements of the still-sleeping garden, however, Beth went up to the third floor, to the room at the end of the hall.

The room had been her mother's workroom when Beth was growing up. The drafting table was still pushed up against the wall, but it was bare and empty. The pencils, papers and watercolors that used to clutter the space were long gone, as was her mother. The memories were there, but tucked away, out of daily reach. Now the room was simply something Beth walked through to get to the great wooden door set in the far wall.

That door led out to a narrow walkway running along the roof-edge of her home.

A widow's walk, it was called. A platform, with waist-high rails all around, that circled the house's two chimneys, and gave Beth an almost unobstructed view of the ocean beyond the boundaries of the small town of Seastone, Massachusetts.

She leaned against the railing, feeling the wind tangle in her sleek black hair and tie it into elf knots.

When she was a little girl, her father would sneak her and her cousin up here. Her mother, working at her sketches, would pretend not to see or hear them as they crept, giggling, past her. They would watch the sailboats in the harbor, and the great fishing boats and tankers passing by much farther out in the green-capped waves.

Beth was older now, her family long gone, and her hair was cut short, above her shoulders, but the wind still tangled it in exactly the same way, as though a giant hand were tousling it.

And she still leaned against the railing of the widow's walk and watched the boats slip by. Only now, rather than feeling a sense of history and contentment when she watched them, Beth felt her restlessness increase until it was an almost physical ache in her legs and arms.

Did everyone feel it, in the quiet pockets of the day when nothing else occupied their minds and bodies? Or was it just her, this strange echoing, like there was something scooped out and hollow inside, when the seasons shifted and the winds changed? She had almost asked friends and total strangers, time and again, when she was away at college in Boston, and after, when she came home, when this whimsical mood attached itself to her. Each time, something had held her back from actually saying something. Fear of an answer, perhaps. Of discovering that yes, it was only her. That only she felt it, and nobody else would ever understand.

Not that it mattered. Each time winter or summer

came, the restlessness passed, and she found purpose and focus again.

"More of the same. Always more of the same." And yet, even as she said it, trying to reassure herself, something deep inside told her that there was more to it this time than simple spring fever. Something that surged inside her like a tidal pool, swirling and wearing at her, matching the physical ache with a pool of longing for...

For what?

Beth didn't know. This spring, for some reason, it was different. Stronger. More painful. Usually standing up here and watching the waves move on the surface of the ocean took the harsh edges off, and a bit of physical activity—a bike ride, a hike along the dunes—dealt with the rest, got her through until it went away.

She wasn't so sure it would be enough, this spring.

Once, her father would somehow sense her mood and swing her by the arms, tossing her into the pile of leaves they had raked up on the sloping backyard, or a pile of new-mown grass. Her cousin Tal, nobody ever called him Talbot, would leap after her, and they would wrestle...her father would laugh so hard he had to sit on the ground to recover, and they would leap on him, and the restlessness would disappear, chased out and forgotten.

Had her father known the same restlessness? If he were still here, would he be able to explain it away, give her the way to deal with it, the words to explain it?

It didn't matter. He wasn't here. All gone: father, mother and Tal, her entire family gone in one split second on a rainy highway nearly fifteen years ago. She was the only one left. The one left behind. Would she feel this way, if they had been spared? Would the feeling of separation, of restlessness be soothed by their presence? Or would it have been worse, knowing for certain that there was no one out there who could understand?

A trill at her hip interrupted her morbid thoughts, and she flipped open her cell phone to answer it. "Jake, hi." Jacob Brown—Jake to his friends, which some days seemed to include every person living in Seastone and the surrounding towns. Open-faced and blue-eyed, with a row of freckles better suited to a ten-year-old and the physique of a high school quarterback.

Five years they had been dating, since the summer they both turned twenty-four and got drunk together while sitting on the seawall at midnight. It wasn't a great love, but it was comfortable, and they knew what to expect from each other. Five years, and neither seemingly eager to move forward, or move away from where they were. Every month for the past year Beth had resolved to end it, and every month Jake agreed with her, and yet they still found themselves having dinner and sex on a regular basis.

There was a lot to be said for stability. For knowing what you would be doing each day, and each night, and with whom, and what was expected of you, and what you could expect of them. Sudden changes had never been good things, for her.

"We still on for dinner?" she asked him, giving in once again to habit.

"Maybe not tonight. Storm's coming up, according to the screens. Looks like it might be a doozy."

A storm might explain her mood. Storms did that to her, when they came in off the ocean. "You afraid of a little rain?" she teased, glad for distraction from her own distraction.

"More likely a lot of wind, which means we're probably going to lose power on half the island." Jake was a Realtor, and the property manager for a number of nearby summer homes. If anything happened, he was the guy who had to deal with it, while the owners were safe and dry on the mainland. "Anyway, you remember what happened the last time we went out in a bad spring storm, at, I might add, your instigation?"

She did. Unlike Jake, she still thought it was funny, smiling now at the memory. How many people could say that they got chased across a beach by an irate and very lost bull seal? It wouldn't actually have hurt them—seals were peaceable creatures, as a rule, unless you got near them during breeding or whelping seasons—but Jake's ego had apparently been bruised something fierce by the experience.

Beth's smile widened. "Point taken, forgive me. All right, no rain-swept walks on the beach. So we'll eat somewhere in town?"

"Look…can we make a rain check? Literally?" He sounded distracted now, and she could hear the clicking of computer keys in the background. He must be checking on his clients, probably scanning the weather networks, too. Multitasking always made him cranky.

Beth looked up at the sky, watching newly arrived clouds scud past, wispy white against the pale blue. It looked innocent enough, but she had grown up watching these skies, learning the warning signs. Storms could come up fast, even when it looked clear, especially in the spring. She should know that by now. "Sure," she said, sighing. It wasn't like it mattered, anyway. Dinner with Jake wasn't going to do anything about her feeling of restlessness. It never did. That was part of the problem.

She listened to his agreement, then ended the call.

She didn't want to reschedule. She didn't want to have dinner with Jake at all, truth be told. She didn't want a casual, comfortable dinner where they talked about things they had talked about for years, until the edges were all worn off and it was soft and easy and no surprises, followed by sex that was… Well, it was nice. Enjoyable. But not surprising. Not…passionate.

She wanted passion tonight. She wanted to have a nice rough tumble in the sheets. Something dirty and sweet, sweaty and ache-inducing. Complete with biting and bruising, thrown clothing, tangled sheets, and no regrets, come the morning.

"Yeah, and that's gonna happen," she said, shaking her head. Jake was a sweet, tender lover. Careful and considerate, always whispering endearments. He was a good man.

He just wasn't The One. Whatever that meant.

Disgusted with herself, Beth rubbed the smooth surface of the teak railing, as though to wipe those treasonous thoughts out of her head, but they wouldn't go.

She was very fond of Jake. He was a great guy. But they were never going to go anywhere except in circles. And after five years...that wasn't enough. They both knew it. And suddenly, right now, the lack made her want to scream.

"Spring fever. That's all. You get it every year." But even as she went inside, closing the door behind her as though to block out the disturbing influences of the salt- and pollen-laden air, Beth knew that there was more to it than that. Something was rising in her, like the storm surge and just as impossible to control.

A glance out the window showed her Jake had been right—the storm was coming in, and coming hard. Even in the half hour since she had left the roof, things had picked up speed. The sea was agitated, churning back and forth, and the sky seemed lower than normal, visibility poor and getting worse. Pity the sailor caught out in this, if they didn't make it home in time. At best they would lose their lunch over the side. At worst...

Worst in a storm could get pretty bad.

Her head was muzzy and stuffed, and her skin felt too tight. Maybe she was coming down with something.

She changed into an old pair of jeans and a thick fleece sweatshirt and went down to the kitchen to make her usual virus-fighting dinner of fresh pasta and vegetables, steamed and tossed with fresh-grated cheese, garlic and cracked pepper, and a beer that she didn't finish. The taste was off, flat and metallic.

"Yeah, probably coming down with a cold. Joy." She poured the beer down the drain, left the dishes in the sink and went back into the office, determined to get something accomplished today other than fretting and woolgathering. A client had sent her a number of old family photos, browned, yellowed and cracked, to be scanned and digitally repaired. Her professional shingle might say Elizabeth Havelock, Photography, but it was this restoration work that kept the mortgage paid and the groceries coming in.

Ten minutes of prep calmed her enough to start working, and another ten minutes into the project, and finally the panacea of work did its job, at least enough for her to forget her fuzzy-headed twitchiness. The whir of the scanner and the clicking of the mouse were soothing as she studied the image on the oversize flat-screen monitor that was her pride and joy, and made minute corrections to the photo, bringing the damaged photograph back to life. There was a crack across the woman's face that slowly mended, half-inch by half-inch. Her world narrowed to the mouse and the screen and the pixels healing like magic under her application. It wasn't art, wasn't groundbreaking, news-making work, but it was satisfying in its own way.

The storm finally broke around 7:00 p.m., with the sudden hard patter of rain on the roof, followed almost immediately by a heavy crack of lightning overhead, and the low, rumbling echo of thunder rolling in from the ocean. The sense of sudden, almost painful relief flooding her body took her by surprise, and her shoulders, which Beth hadn't even realized were hunched while she worked, relaxed immediately. She looked out the single window in the studio. Branches bowed and waved in the wind, and water splattered against the window, echoing from every pane in the house.

Storms sounded different out here than they did on the mainland. Hell, storms *were* different. When it rained in Boston, when she was in college, it never felt this…soothing.

Thunder crashed again, and she shook her head. "And that puts an end to that for the evening," she said, shutting down her computer once everything was backed up. You didn't take chances with the electronics in an old house during a spring storm, especially when those electronics represented your livelihood.

No sooner had she thought that than the over-head lights flickered, came back on and then went out. The familiar steady hum she barely heard anymore died as well, leaving the house in an almost supernatural stillness broken only by the rain.

"Jinx," she muttered. Well, she was officially off the clock now. Mother Nature insisted.

In the drawer of her desk there was a flashlight, and she used it to find her way to the store of candles, the sound of thick, heavy raindrops on the roof and windows following her as she went through the house. The linen closet on the second floor was the repository of all blackout supplies— extra gallons of water, a box of protein bars, dry shampoo and soap, and an entire shelf filled with thick pillar candles.

Beth's practical streak failed her when it came to candles. These were handmade by a local crafts-woman, lilac in color and scented with clean, crisp lavender and sea grass. Picking three of the candles off the shelf, along with a book of matches, she closed the closet door and went back downstairs to the main parlor. It had always been her favorite room, aside from the corner bedroom that had been hers all her life, and if the storm was going to go all night, then that was where she would wait it out.

One pillar went on the walnut coffee table, one on the plaster mantel over the fireplace and the third she positioned on the table next to the old cracked leather sofa. Using only one match to light them all, the room was soon bathed in a warm, comforting light. There was something about the flickering of candle flame that she adored; it didn't fill the room the way artificial light did, but it seemed to illumi-

nate better, somehow. The antiques in the room
looked better in firelight: her great-grandfather's
spyglass; the rough but gorgeous little carvings of
ivory that dated back to when whaling was the
industry on this island; the handmade wooden ships
her father had collected, three- and two-masters, all
perfect down to the last detail, including the narrow
boats lashed to their sides. Neither she nor Tal had
ever felt the desire to play with them when they
were children. They would watch them for hours,
but never once had she taken one down other than
to dust or display it for someone else. It was as
though it was forbidden to look too closely, to ask
too much, although her parents had never forbidden her or Tal anything of the sort.

Now, in the candlelight, she watched the shadows
their masts and riggings made on the cream-painted
walls, and felt some of her restlessness subside.
Those boats were her inheritance, as much as this
house; they told the story of her great-grandfather
helping to build the fleets that used to ply these
waters, her grandfather's specialization in the car-
pentry of higher-end boats that put her dad through
college, and her own dad's fascination with boats
that never seemed to translate into anything larger
than those models. An entire family, tied to the
shoreline without ever actually going out to sea.
Beth suddenly wondered why she felt no particular
draw toward boats, why Tal had actually gotten
seasick the one time he went out on a fishing boat
when they were in grade school. Maybe it was some-

thing genetic, and the further from their shipbuilding great-grandfather you got, the less you cared?

"Maybe it was just the storm," she said. "Maybe I need a vacation. Get off the island for a little bit. Maybe go inland, see a forest or a mountain." She had never gone more than a day's travel inland; there were entire stretches of the country she had never seen except as the backdrop for movies on the television. Maybe she could get a passport, leave the country. See England, or Paris, or...

Her imagination failed her. She didn't have a passport. She'd never been on a plane. She didn't even watch the Travel Channel, for God's sake. "Maybe it's time to change all of that," she said. "Do something different."

A crack of thunder and a flash of lightning directly overhead sounded as though in answer.

"Fine, but is that a yes or a no?" she asked the ceiling, half expecting a reply. But the lights stayed off, the rain came down and no further electrical energy exploded overhead.

"Thanks for nothing," she said, curling up on the sofa, her arms around her knees. Her attention was drawn, not to the shadows now, or even the fireplace, laid with wood already in case she wanted one last fire before warmer weather came in, but into the next room, where a plate-glass window looked out over the small front yard, over the tops of smaller Cape-style houses, down the road that led to the shoreline.

There were lights flickering outside, on the road

heading toward the beach. Most of them were white headlights, but—she squinted—at least one or two were red. Cops. Or an ambulance.

There wasn't anything she could do, if there had been an accident, either some idiot in a car, or a greater idiot in a boat. She had the basics of CPR, courtesy of a town-wide push last summer, but she wasn't a paramedic or anything useful. There was nothing she could do at the scene other than clutter it up and get herself soaked. There was no reason she was extinguishing the candles, grabbing the flashlight, an oiled baseball cap and her raincoat, and grabbing the keys to her Toyota.

No reason at all. Except a sudden need to be there, to see what the storm had brought in.

The rain almost knocked her little car to the side of the road a time or two, but she got to the beach without disaster. The rain and clouds made it seem much later in the evening, closer to midnight than 8:00 p.m., and added to the unreality of the entire scene, to Beth. There were dark forms on the sand, over the dunes: people gathered, and a single vehicle with the red lights on top that marked it as belonging to the rescue squad.

Not an accident, then. Not a car, anyway. And no sign of wreckage that you'd expect, if someone were stupid enough to take a boat out with a storm coming in…

She parked and got out, startled by how noisy the rain was, once she was in it. Cold and hard, and even through her rain slicker she was quickly drenched.

The cap kept the water off her face, but nothing more than that, and her hair stuck to her scalp unpleasantly.

"Get the stretcher over here!" a man's voice yelled. "And you people, back off! You'd think you'd never seen a moron before."

"Never one out of uniform" the retort came back from one of the bystanders, a woman. Beth slowed her steps a little. Obviously, whoever it was was still alive, and not in critical danger, if they were mouthing off over his body. Nobody here was quite hardened enough to crack jokes over a dead body. Something prickled on the back of her neck, like a spider walking there, or the unexpected touch of a warm hand. She flinched, and then looked around, feeling embarrassed, but there wasn't anything but the crowd gathered, seven or eight people, including herself. And yet, somehow, the feeling remained, like some phantom hand rested just above her collar.

It wasn't like her to spook at anything, much less nothing. After one last look around, she shrugged off the feeling and turned to the much more real scene in front of her.

"Evening, Beth." The nearest dark form in rain hat and slicker turned out to be Mrs. Daley, who had taught seventh-grade math to Beth and her cousin, with variable success. She was in her sixties now, but still held students in thrall with a voice of steel and a heart of marshmallow.

"What happened?" Beth asked her.

"No idea. The call went out from the lighthouse about an hour ago—they spotted something in the water. So we came out to search."

"We" in this case was the self-titled border patrol, a group of locals who came out when a whale or dolphin beached itself, or a ship got into trouble, or any other crisis requiring a pair of hands and a strong back. Mrs. Daley was a charter member.

"And found…"

"One body, male." Mrs. Daley leaned in, laughter in her voice even if Beth couldn't see her face clearly in the dusk and rain. "Nude."

"Mrs. Daley!" Beth had to laugh, and immediately felt bad about it. "He's all right, though?"

The older woman nodded. "Out cold, but doesn't seem to be anything wrong with him. In any sense of the word. Spoilsport Josiah had to go and throw a blanket over him, though. Poor boy. I hope there wasn't anyone else out there with him."

Beth assumed that she meant the stranger, not Josiah. "A boat wreck, then?"

"Well, what else could it be, wash him up here, a night like tonight? No debris, that anyone's seen, but you think he was just out for a casual swim? In that water?"

The Atlantic Ocean was not a gentle body of water, even in summer. It was only spring now, which meant that the water was still too cold for anyone but the most fervent polar bear or long-distance swimmer to be out in it. Although you never knew what someone from Away, a non-Islander, might do; people came here and did stupid things, all the time. Usually in tourist season, though.

Beth felt that prickle again, this time all down her spine, and she shivered. Not a warm hand this time; more like the sleek dark shadow of something swimming in the deep waters below her.

The crowd parted, and she could see that the paramedics were loading him onto the stretcher now. Drawn by the same urgency that got her down there, Beth moved forward, needing for some reason to see the face of this stranger.

"Miss, stay back, please." She didn't know the paramedic; he must have been new. Not that she knew everyone in town—it was small but not that small—but almost everyone was on nodding basis with everyone else.

That thought put the words in her mouth. "I...want to make sure I don't know him."

It wasn't totally a lie. She did want to make sure of that. She didn't think there was a chance in hell she did know him, but it worked; the paramedic moved aside just enough for her to see the guy's face in the light of the emergency vehicle's head-lights.

Pale skin, even allowing for shock and being washed out under those flashing red lights. Clean-shaven, with broad, strong cheekbones. Masculine, without being heavy or brutish. The light flickered, highlighting reddish glints in thick black hair so

much like hers—there was a moment of shock, and
Beth felt her knees almost give out under her.

"Ma'am?" The paramedic was right there at her
elbow. "Do you know him?"

That moment of concern allowed her to get close
enough to touch the stranger, the flesh of one arm
outside the blanket, wet from seawater and rain,
cold but not dead-cold, just wet-cold.

"No." Her breath came back in a rush, and her
heart started beating again. No, it wasn't Tal. It wasn't
her cousin, dead and buried and not haunting her because he would never have been cruel enough to do
that. Just some guy with hair the same color and texture his had been, like hers, that was all. Coincidence.

And the look of this guy said he was closer to her
age, maybe in his early thirties at most, than Tal's
fifteen when he died. Beth swallowed and forced
herself to look again. The features were different, too,
now that she could see him more clearly. Tal had been
blessed with the family nose, a sort of turned-up snub,
and his skin had been darker, his coloring inherited
from his Italian father, not the pale-as-flounder
Havelock line. This stranger was pale like that, like
she was, and his nose was longer, narrower, his mouth
wider, the chin more stubborn, and without the five-
o'clock shadow that Tal got, even as a teenager.

She touched the stranger's arm again, driven by
an urge that she didn't understand, and something
sparked under her fingers, making her shiver again
from something other than the cold.

Something clicked. Something changed, here

and now. Chemicals collided in her bloodstream,
stars aligned, a wave crested and fell, and she was
never going to be the same again.

Beth shook her head, refusing the sense of por-
tent overwhelming her. She didn't believe in that
sort of thing—she was tired, that was all. Tired
enough to swear that the guy was shimmering in the
rain, that his skin was overlaid with something,
some kind of…

A second layer, almost. The kind that she used
when she was retouching photographs, to blank out
details she didn't want to use in the final product or
distract the eye from things that couldn't be repaired.

Beth blinked, then wiped at her eyes with the
back of her hand. Humans couldn't be retouched.
She was probably running a fever to go with her
cold; that would explain it. She needed to get the
hell out of the rain, get her overtired imagination
under control.

"No," she said again, backing away before she
could touch the body again. "I don't know him."

They bundled the stretcher into the ambulance
and pulled away slowly over the sand, lights flashing but the siren off. The crowd started to drift
away, and Beth drifted with it, back to the house.
She shed her raincoat and sneakers just inside the
door, then peeled off her sodden jeans and sweater
as well, and walked through the house in damp
panties and socks. The main bathroom upstairs was
old-fashioned enough to still have the original claw-
foot tub, and she started the water running hot while

she stripped off her socks and underwear and added scented bath salts to the water. Hair piled on top of her head, she sank gratefully into the steaming, sweet-smelling water up to her shoulders and felt her body finally let go of the rain's chill. She reached up with her toes and managed to shut the tap off before the water reached a dangerously overfull level. Her muscles softened, her eyes closed, and only some remnant of awareness kept her from falling asleep in the tub. When the water cooled enough to rouse her, she hauled her body out of the tub, dried off and put on warm flannel pajamas and slid into bed. The moment her damp head hit the pillow, she was asleep, dreaming of deep green waves, briny air and the slide of warm, warm hands along the inside of her legs and up across her stomach, lingering in places that made her smile in her sleep, as she turned to embrace her pillow as though it were a lover.

Chapter 2

He woke slowly, surfacing with a sense of panic blunted by something soft and sticky.

There was dark and a sudden shock of pain, and…nothing. He opened his eyes, his lashes gummy and stuck together, and discovered that he was in a bed. He knew it was a bed, although he hadn't slept in one since he was a child, preferring a hammock that mimicked the motion of the waves.

A bed. In a place he didn't recognize, filled with smells he didn't recognize.

There were no windows wherever he was, only a single narrow doorway. White surrounded him, white sheets and walls, and shiny metals and plastics and that overwhelming smell of something that made his nostrils flare in distrust and disgust.

Cleansers, part of his brain reminded him. To clean up the shit and the blood. You're in a hospital.

He had been in one of those, long ago. His sister had torn open her leg on a rusty nail half-submerged off a dock, and she'd had to go to the mainland and have it stitched up. As her favorite sibling, her only brother, closest in age, he had gone with her and their mother, to keep her calm while the doctors did their thing. There had been the same smells, and shots, and the adults had all been annoyed but not really worried.

That was good. Annoyed but not worried meant this was an inconvenience, not a threat. Hospitals were where they helped you. What was this hospital helping him for? What had he done to himself? Nothing hurt, nothing felt wrong.... It annoyed him that he couldn't remember.

"Good morning."

He turned his head and looked up at a man who was pushing back the curtains and moving to stand beside the bed. An older man, maybe even Elder. Gray hair and beard; the latter was cut into a sharp point on his chin, like a shark's fin. But the eyes were pale blue and kind.

"Morning," he responded, his voice raspy, like he'd been yelling. Maybe he had. He couldn't remember even that much.

"I don't suppose you could tell me your name?"

He could. He could remember that. But it wouldn't mean much to this man, his name and colony-connection, identifying him as seal-kin.

Nothing this human male could understand. An instant of panic flooded his brain, and then another name came to him from memories of long ago, names and connections to the land...

"Dylan." He coughed, spoke again more firmly, confidence coming back to him with the memories. "My name's Dylan. Dylan...Meridith."

"Excellent." The man took a thin instrument out of his white coat's pocket and flicked it on, a narrow beam of light coming from one end. Dylan obediently let him flick the light into one eye and then the other, relieved when the man—a doctor?—grunted in satisfaction and turned the light off. "Look this way, please? And that way. Excellent. No headache? Very good. Lie back now, and relax. You gave us all quite a scare, Mr. Meridith, washing up like that. Usually by the time the Atlantic gets done with bodies, they go to the morgue, not the emergency room."

He had been swimming, that was right. Heading for shore. Looking...

Looking for his mate. Yes.

Dylan lay back on the pillow, the memories returning now. Bypassing the other colonies to come here, to where humans lived, this arm of land jutting out from the mainland. Swimming, endlessly swimming: so focused that he ignored the warning signs of the storm, when he should have known better. The storm came. Waves knocking him over, being bumped by something, losing consciousness...

And waking up here.

"I... You found me on the sand." It wasn't a question; he remembered that, vaguely. Voices and lights, things being done to his body, bringing his temperature back up... He owed those people his life. "Thank you."

"You're welcome. Although I had the easy part, just waiting for you to wake up." He smiled, and the kind blue eyes sparkled with life and humor. "I'm Dr. Alden, by the way, and I'm the one who says when you get to go home. But first, we need to know where home is, exactly."

Dylan froze. The name he'd given the doctor had been placed in his memory years ago, just in case, but he hadn't thought of what to say about his home. He hadn't even thought to think about it.

He trusted this Dr. Alden, instinctively. Despite that, his voice caught before any words escaped. You never told where the colony was. You never betrayed the kin living there. That was the first training seal-kin got, when they first went out among the human-kin. It was too dangerous.

Sometimes, following instinct was good. Sometimes, it was not so good. What was he supposed to do?

Another flash of memory: someone talking over him, something about debris, looking for debris, of...a boat?

"Daughter of the Sea," he said, buying time with whatever came to mind. "My boat. Is it okay?"

Since there wasn't any such boat, he wasn't horribly crushed when Dr. Alden sadly told him that there was no sign of his boat anywhere, not even debris. But it gave him enough time to come up with a story that would get him out of this hospital.

Because he remembered something else from the night before, after the feel of sand under his face and being wrapped in blankets and bundled into a vehicle. He remembered a warm voice, and a cool hand on his skin, and the reaction he'd had, even mostly unconscious, to her presence.

A woman. The woman he had come to find.

She was here.

He had come to the right place, after all. The sea had not betrayed him.

Dr. Alden excused himself and disappeared beyond the curtains, leaving Dylan to sink into the hard comfort of his bed. She was *here*.

And with that thought, the urgency returned, a wave that would have knocked him over were he not already lying down. Instead, it sent him bolt upright.

He had to find her. Now.

"Where do you think you're going, young man?"

The doctor appeared next to him, a firm hand on his arm. Dylan would have protested except that he feared, if the human let go, he would fall on his face like a weanling denied milk.

"You said I was fine."

"I said you hadn't suffered any permanent damage. That's not fine. You were badly dehydrated, battered, and unless I miss my guess, your muscles aren't responding very well to commands even now."

"I'll be fine. I…" This doctor had eyes like
Dylan's grandfather: wide-set, sky-blue and gentle,
but still able to see through any lie you might even
think about telling. "I mean no disrespect, sir. I
know that you mean well. But I don't like being
indoors, especially in a medical facility. I'd do better
if I could find a place with…with windows, at
least."

"Humph." The doctor's gruff voice didn't match
the understanding in those eyes, and Dylan felt
himself relax, even as the older man ushered him
back onto the bed.

"I'll tell you what. You let me run a few tests,
make me feel better about turning you out into the
street, and I'll sign off on your discharge papers
today. Deal?"

Dylan nodded. "Deal."

Part of the test involved giving up quantities of
his blood, and breathing into a strange device of
three tubes with small balls inside. Dylan amused
himself by making all three balls rise and fall in
unison, until Doctor Alden admitted that his lungs
were in excellent shape and took the device away.
Then, he had to walk the length of the clinic—ten
beds and two exam rooms—without faltering.

A glimpse out the one window in the hallway, a
single clear pane of glass, reassured him that he was
not far from the sea—set on a rise of land, the clinic
looked over rooftops toward the wide expanse of
water. Dr. Alden left him there, staring out at the
horizon, while he went off to do whatever it was

that doctors did. Soon enough the nurse came by and shooed him back to his bed, where a pair of dark blue pants, a white shirt and cheap white sneakers waited. "Your clothing didn't survive your wreck," she said apologetically. "We had to guess at your size and the color choices were, well, limited."

"Thank you." He had left home so quickly, without thinking anything through, he hadn't even thought about clothing. Or money. Oh, hell.

He dropped the simple robe and reached for the jeans. The nurse let out a noise that was a cross between a giggle and a squeak, and left him to get dressed.

"So." Dr. Alden appeared without fanfare as he was lacing up the shoes. "No dizziness? No last-minute headache to crash your escape plans?"

"I'm good?" Dylan waited with bated breath for the answer.

"You're annoyingly good. If all of my patients healed up as quickly as you did, I'd be out of business and have to find honest work."

The nurse walking by snickered quietly, then ducked her head when the doctor mock-glared at her. "You can see that I get no respect at all, already."

Dylan wisely stayed out of the argument. At home, females outnumbered males 3:2 and bossed the younger males around mercilessly, giving way only when males reached what his mother called "the interesting age." That snicker had sounded re-

assuringly familiar to a man who grew up surrounded by sisters.

"All right. Yes, you get your walking papers, and
consider yourself a lucky son of a bitch. Try to keep
on top of the water, not under it, from now on?"

Dylan merely smiled and took the papers the
doctor handed him, scrawling something on the
line for his own signature. His people spent almost
half their lives riding underneath the waves. But he
appreciated the concern.

Dr. Alden put his own signature on the papers
that made his release official and tucked them into
his clipboard. "There you go. I want you to check
in with your own doctor when you get home,
though, just to be on the safe side. All right?"

"I had actually planned on staying in town for a
little while," Dylan admitted. "It seems like a nice
place. From the little I saw of it last night."

Dr. Alden laughed. "Watery and dark, you mean.
It is a nice enough place, yes. We avoid the worst
of the tourist invasion, and I certainly like it here,
but I can't imagine there'd be much to keep you
occupied, unless you're here for the beach or the
views. Still, if you're going to stay, welcome to
you. And feel free to stop by if anything at all feels
odd or uneasy."

"I will. Ah…" Dylan suddenly felt awkward
again. Free. Nothing in the human world was free,
and he had no money. Nothing at all, except… The
weight on his ankle was a sudden, reassuring
shock—the anklet, a gift from his sister years

before, was so familiar he had forgotten it was there. He could sell that, maybe. Sell it, and settle his debt.

"Don't worry about it, young Dylan." Dr. Alden's eyes were kind again. "Men who show up stark naked on our beach, and don't immediately ask for a phone to call their family? We don't expect you're going to pull out a platinum card. Fortunately, you weren't exactly a financial burden, not needing much more than a bed and treatment for mild dehydration and exhaustion."

"Still, I…"

"Someday, when you can, you'll make a donation. Yes?"

"Yes." He would. Even if he had to swim all the way back from the colony with the funds clenched between his teeth, he would.

"Do you have somewhere to stay? Tourist town, Nantucket's become. No decent place cheap anymore. But you go to the Blue Anchor. I'll call ahead, and Brandt will take care of you for a few days, until you figure things out."

Seals were communal, and so by default were their kin. But they tended to care only for their own, and strangers were not welcomed. Humans, it seemed, were different. That pleased Dylan, even as it confused him slightly. If they knew how very much a stranger he was, would they still welcome him? Or would they drive him out?

Instinct warned him to stay silent, to try to fit in as quickly and quietly as possible. There was so much he didn't know, so many ways he could do the wrong thing. He wasn't used to being uncertain. It pissed him off, both the sensation and the hesitation.

Leaving the clinic, the sharp scent of sea and salt slid into his pores and made his muscles relax after the antiseptic feel of the clinic. The sun was warm overhead, white clouds scudding against a clear blue sky, and the sound of gulls soaring and screaming overhead was like laughter in his ears.

A full day waited in front of him. A full day, and his mate waiting for him, somewhere nearby. The thought that she might be within earshot, even, her silken skin waiting for his touch…

The rush of blood to his groin wasn't unexpected. The strange tightness in his chest was more of a surprise. He tried to breathe normally, remembering how easy it had been to breathe into the medical apparatus, but the tightness remained. It wasn't his lungs that weren't working, but the muscles in his chest, constricting around his heart with a pang that felt a little like hunger, and a little like sadness.

When he claimed his mate, all those emotions would go away. The knowledge came to him the same way awareness of her had, appearing like something he'd always known only never consciously realized until now. He had to find her. Everything would be all right once he found her.

But first, he needed to find a place that would buy his anklet. A jewelry store, or a crafts stall. Or a pawnshop. Something like that, any town of decent size would have to have those, yes? Then, he would go to this bed-and-breakfast. It burned him to take charity, but maybe, if he got enough for the anklet, he wouldn't have to. Money was the first priority, though. He might be willing to sleep on the beach without fuss, but if he was going to look among humans, he needed to stay among them, too.

Glancing down at the sheet of paper Dr. Alden had given him, with a rough-drawn map and a name on it, he stepped onto the sidewalk, and started moving toward his goal.

Chapter 3

Beth had woken early that morning, listening to the birds doing their welcome-the-dawn thing outside her window, and cautiously probed her emotional status the way a bomb technician might inspect a suspicious package. Yes, still twitchy, even though the storm had blown through, and the skies were now clear and bright. In fact, she thought that it might even be worse now, and she couldn't blame it on the weather.

Or the dream she'd had, all sea-green and salty, the pressure on her lungs as though she were holding her breath too long, like being held underwater but without any of the fear or agitation you might think would come from a dream about drowning.

She knew how to swim, of course. You didn't grow up on an island and not know how to swim. But her family was odd among the Nantucket old-timers; nobody in her family went to sea for their career. Not back when there was an actual sailing-and-whaling industry based on the island, not to the navy, marines, or Coasties—although there were stories of a distant cousin in the air force, during WWII—and not now. Hell, they didn't even own a boat, relying on the ferry to get them the short distance between the island and mainland. They stayed put on land, and did landy things—without ever getting too far from the ocean itself. She tried to remember a single close relative who had moved to a landlocked state, and failed. She had gone away for college, but come home as soon as she could, and her father had never even gotten that far away, and every cousin within two generations had been the same.

So why was she now dreaming of the sea like it was something she had been missing all her life? How could you yearn for something you always had, and never particularly wanted?

It had been an erotic dream, too, she remembered now, stretching and blushing slightly at the memory. Waves like hands stroking her skin, the water blood-warm, even as her blood warmed more. Her own hand slid down her belly, tangling briefly in the curls between her legs, curls that were still damp from the intensity of that dream.

Beth let out a deep sigh and scrubbed at her face

with both hands, trying to erase all images, erotic or otherwise, from her head. "That storm just messed with you, is all. The storm, and that naked man on the beach...

"Oh, yeah. Time to get out of the house, away from the darkroom and the computer and all the stress, and put some fresh air on your face," she told herself, throwing off the covers and making her way, shivering, to the wardrobe. Never mind that it hadn't worked all that well yesterday; today was a new day. Anything was possible, right?

Underwear, a pair of sweats and a jog bra, and a windbreaker over that, two pairs of socks, and her sneakers, and she was ready to go. Ten minutes later, she had pulled her bike out of storage and was pedaling down the road, already feeling her mood improve even as the memory of the dream faded. The road was slick with morning dew, and the air was crisp and salty on her skin, just the way it should be. Instead of heading to the beach road as usual, though, she went upland, above town, and away from the water. It was more of a workout that way, she justified to herself, feeling her muscles protest as she headed up a steep incline. If she worked hard this morning, she could eat an éclair from Peggie's Bakery after dinner without guilt.

Maybe even two, if she only had a salad for dinner itself.

An hour later, sweating and grinning, éclairs earned and her mood on a definite upswing, she locked the bike up outside the local diner and went inside.

"Morning, Miss Elizabeth," the man behind the counter called out. "Coffee 'n' eggroll?"

"Please, yes, thank you, Ben." The eggroll had been a joke since she was ten—it was exactly that, a hard roll with scrambled eggs inside. No bacon, no ham, nothing except egg, to which Beth would add a dose of hot sauce just before she ate it. The first time she had gone to a Chinese restaurant, the notion that there might be another kind of egg roll had completely floored her.

She sat at the counter, since there wasn't anyone else in the diner except a trucker at one of the tables, staring into his coffee like it held the answer to everything. After dumping her bike helmet on the seat next to her, she propped her elbows up on the Formica counter and waited for the coffee and inevitable…

"Didja heah about the guy washed up on the beach?"

Glory not only made the best eggroll in the world, she also knew everything that happened in town, often before the people it was happening to knew. She should have been a reporter for the *Times,* not a short-order cook.

Beth looked at the square-shouldered woman, her gray curls pulled into a ponytail that should have looked ridiculous on a woman her age, but somehow worked. She and her husband, Ben, had owned the diner since before Beth was born, and she suspected they'd be here long after she had

died. They were just so…solid. Like granite under-
foot, only not so heavy, since neither Glory nor Ben
were very large individuals. In fact, Ben was shorter
than Beth was, and couldn't weigh much more than
she did, soaking wet, for all that he gave off a reassuring impression of solidity. When her parents had
died, and there hadn't been anyone else to take the
teenage Elizabeth in, those two had stepped forward, fostering her until she could be on her own,
so that she didn't have to leave her home. She owed
them a debt they refused to even acknowledge. The
least she could do was indulge Glory's love of
gossip.

"I was there," she told Glory. "On the beach last
night when they found him."

"Yes, but did you heah?"

Beth sighed. Obviously, there was more to the
story, and Glory wasn't going to be satisfied until
she had the telling of it. "I need coffee before
anything else," she told the older woman, pretend-
ing that something inside her hadn't done a weird
flip at the mention of the stranger.

Suddenly, she wasn't sure that she wanted more
coffee after all. That flip feeling wasn't good. Nothing that made her feel like her world was being
turned upside down and roundabout like that could
be any good.

Glory, unaware of Beth's sudden mood change,
was already pouring the black liquid into a thick
white mug and pushing it across the counter into the
younger woman's unresisting hands.

"All right." Beth sighed, her fingers curling around the mug despite herself. There wasn't any graceful way to escape. "Spill all."

"His name's Dylan, he's been checked out of the clinic already and Doc, as usual, refused to take any money for it. That man is going to run himself into the ground, he doesn't watch it."

The rant about Doc Alden was familiar territory, and Glory skipped over it to the new and interesting material. "The boy, Dylan, he was sailing, a boat called the *Daughter of the Sea,* all by himself although nobody seems to know out of what port. Boat's gone now, obviously, not even flinders to be found."

"Lucky guy," Ben muttered, coming behind Glory with a menu for someone who had just come in, and Beth nodded in agreement. A boat that thoroughly destroyed, the captain didn't usually survive.

"He's taken a room at the Blue Anchor for don't know how long. Paid in cash, too. Sold a nice piece of jewelry over at Rosen Jewelers to pay for it. Hasn't called anyone since he's been here, poor boy. Must not have any family. Can you imagine that—" Glory stopped, suddenly aware that Beth would be all too able to imagine that.

"And I'm a thoughtless idiot, but you knew that already. I'm sorry, baby. Here, have some more coffee and I'll go make your eggroll."

Beth couldn't take offense, not from Glory. Despite the efforts of her friends, she had been alone for so long, sometimes she forgot what it was like to be part of even a small larger group. Sometimes. Most of the time it didn't bother her.

Mostly.

"She forgot to tell you that he was single," Ben said, sliding up to the counter and taking right over where his wife left off. "Or at least, no ring and not talking about a wife and kidlets." He had a mug of coffee in his own hands, except that, unlike Beth, this was probably his sixth or seventh mug since the diner had opened at five that morning. Even when he was outside the diner, there was always a to-go cup of coffee somewhere near Ben.

"Probably because I'm not interested?" Beth offered, smiling despite herself.

Ben had known her since she was in the womb, and had been speaking his mind about her personal life since then. "Uh-huh. When was the last time you and Jake made the bed shake?"

"None of your damn business, you pervert," she shot back, refusing to blush or blink.

"I rest my case." Ben looked too damn pleased with himself for a guy who had just pointed out that her social life sucked. She resisted the urge to stick her tongue out at him. Ben was the only person she knew who could make her revert back to being a ten-year-old just by poking her.

"Here you go." Glory returned with a platter of eggroll and a side of hash browns. "Benjamin, you leave the girl alone. You know better than to meddle."

"He does?" That was news to Beth.

Glory knocked her husband affectionately on the shoulder. "You'll come to your senses on your own schedule, or not at all. Nothing we can do to rush it along without making things worse. Now eat. If I know you, you haven't eaten a thing since, oh, lunch yesterday?"

She had, actually, but in the aftermath of the storm and her dreams, she wasn't sure if she could remember what, and Beth suspected Glory would say a meal you didn't remember didn't count.

She ate, and Ben and Glory both left her alone, disappearing back into the chrome-and-white depths of the diner's kitchen.

Her own schedule? Schedule for what? On any other day the comment would have washed right over her, but today it stuck at her restlessness like a burr, and itched in a place she couldn't quite reach. She and Jake might not have been setting the world on fire, but what did that have to do with a schedule?

And if Glory or Ben made one single comment about biological clocks ticking, she was going to clean *their* clocks. Of all the things she ever wanted in her life, gotten or not gotten, kids were not on the list. She wasn't even much for pets, although her mother had fed stray cats in the neighborhood. They had all slipped away in the year after the accident; she had forgotten that, too. So much, she had made herself forget.

The eggroll satisfied her stomach, but the contentment she had earned slipped away, leaving her feeling irritable and restless all over again. What was here for her, really? Okay, the family house, and people who had known her since her mother went into the hospital to give birth, but…so what? Things that normally made her feel supported and secure now added to her irritation.

Maybe it was time, finally, to do something different. Maybe that was what this restlessness was about. Maybe…maybe she would paint the house pink. Or black. Black, with hot-pink trim.

The thought of what her proper New Englander neighbors would say made her feel slightly better, even as she knew she would do no such thing. It wasn't a Havelock thing to do, to draw attention to herself, or her house. Not that there was any rule against it, or that she had ever been scolded for making a fuss, it just…wasn't Done. The family had lived generations on this island and managed to stay out of every single history book or pamphlet, after all. Her dad used to pretend to be annoyed by that, but she got a sense of satisfaction from him, too. Like he had managed to pull off some secret trick nobody knew about… It was another thing they had never talked about. She had been too young, too full of herself then, to think her father might have anything she needed to know.

Not for the first time, she wondered what she might have learned, if they'd lived long enough for her to listen.

"Be a love, will you?" Ben was back, Glory glaring at him over the transom where the orders were placed. He handed her a brown-wrapped package. "Drop this off for me in town?"

"Town" was a two-block walk away from the diner. Ben walked the two miles from their cottage to the diner every morning, no matter the weather, to start the kitchen before dawn. He was hardly in need of assistance.

Beth narrowed her hazel-green eyes at him, but he maintained a look of perfect innocence.

She studied the address on the package's label. It was addressed to someone in Rockport, Maine, and was already stamped and ready to go. Ben could have just left it out on the counter for the postman to pick up during his rounds.

"What game are you playing, Benjamin?" she wondered, and got only a low chuckle from behind the counter. Beth slid the package to the side, away from her coffee, and went to work on her breakfast. If she was going to be chore-girl, she was going to be fed, first. Post office was barely open yet, anyway. And it was off-season—not like there would be a line.

The bedroom Dylan had been shown to on the third floor of the three-story house was large, by his standards, with a bed, a pedestal sink and a book-case filled with old books. Normally, as a single male, he didn't stay under a roof unless the weather was particularly bad, and the peaked, plastered ceiling meeting his gaze was not as pretty as the flat, wood-beamed one he and his father had rebuilt after a nor'easter almost destroyed the seal-kin village, but it seemed to suit the building. Wooden flooring was covered by a rug made out of brightly colored bits of cloth. His mother had a rug like that in her own cottage, and for a moment Dylan felt his throat close up with an unfamiliar sensation.

Loneliness, he identified it, without too much surprise. Well, he was without colony or cousins in this place, it made sense. Not pleasant, but understandable.

But the knowledge that his mate waited for him somewhere in this village made the sensation pass. Once he found her, they could return home, and all would be right again.

And surely seal-kin came up on these shores. Maybe he wouldn't be entirely alone here, during his search?

With that thought, he pushed open the single window, enjoying the feel of the crisp morning air on his skin, looking out into a beautiful blue sky he'd been too focused before then to notice. No clouds, only the slightest hint of any moisture at all in the air, a fine day for swimming…

Or finding a mate.

Single-minded, aren't you? He could hear his mother's voice, laughing at him. He really should have said something to her, at least, before he left. But nothing to be done for it now. She would at least know—or suspect—where he had gone, and why. He had always been given to acting on impulse.

Dylan took off the sneakers and shucked the

clothing the nurse had given him, dropping them on the bed and luxuriating in the feel of the air through the open window on his skin.

The pull was getting stronger, minute by minute, until it was becoming almost painful. Worse than pain, worse than hunger or lust, even though there was something of both to it. He thought about relieving himself of the lust, at least, but something stopped his hand on the first stroke. There was no shame in pleasure, but…he didn't want to take it alone. Not when he was so close to finding Her.

Dylan was struck with an intense urge to take a shower, to wash the last stink of the hospital off his skin. He ran a hand through his hair, feeling the dry texture of it with displeasure. They had washed it for him at the clinic, while he was unconscious, but used some sort of soap that took the natural oils out, so the strands felt brittle. Worse, his skin felt almost as dry; he wasn't used to spending this much time out of the water. Not that he couldn't—one of his sisters used to routinely go off for months at a time when she went to college, and his oldest brother worked on an oil rig, where shedding your human form to go diving into the ocean at a moment's whim was not exactly a good idea. But Dylan was used to spending most of his time with his cousins, in his other skin. Being caught in human form endlessly was…itchy.

He looked out the window again, judging how far this building was from the shoreline, then shrugged and went in search of the shared bathroom down the hall he had been shown the night before. A good soak in a tub wouldn't be the same, but it would get him clean, anyway.

A low scream made him jump back into his room, slamming the door shut behind him. His heart pounding, Dylan tried to determine where the threat was coming from. Then he looked down, and a red flush stained his pale skin.

He had forgotten for a moment that he wasn't home, and had gone outside without any clothing.

"Sorry," he called out to the unsuspecting fellow guest in the hallway, reaching out to grab the drawstring blue pants and drag them back up his legs. "Wasn't quite awake yet."

By the time he made it downstairs, his skin comfortably soaked and his black hair slicked back away from his face, the woman he had startled and two other guests were in quiet conversation—about him, clearly, from the laughter that broke out when he appeared. Dylan felt himself blush again, and a wave of irritation followed. It had been an easy enough mistake to make; he wasn't exactly used to wearing clothing, after all. At home, people were more comfortable with skin, theirs and others', in any form.

"Glad you could join us," Mr. Brandt—Mike— said, only a trace of teasing in his voice, although he was clearly hard-pressed to keep from smiling. "I held over some food from breakfast, as Doc Alden said you'd probably be hungry. Breads and whatnot are on the buffet, and everything else is family-style on the table."

"Everything else" included a platter of salmon piled high and red, and what looked like smoked chub, and Dylan felt his mouth start to water. He hadn't realized how hungry he was. The rest of the foods—scrambled eggs, bacon and fresh fruits— were added to his plate more cautiously. They were treats to his people, not everyday meals, and he was almost afraid to take too much, for fear of doing something wrong, or rude.

"How are you feeling?" Mike asked, reaching over to drop another two slices of the crisp pork onto his plate with a wink. "Doc says you were pretty beat up when they brought you in, but you look fine now."

"More exhausted than anything else. They warned me I may be sleeping a lot for a while, to recover."

"So what are your plans today?" Mike asked as Dylan sat down at the table with his plate. "Other than clothes shopping?"

That started everyone laughing again, and even Dylan, despite his blush, acknowledged now that it was amusing.

"I really don't know," he said. "Get my bearings, figure out what I'm going to do."

"Have they found any trace of your boat?"

It took Dylan a moment to remember what boat the woman was talking about, then remembered his lie to the doctor. Another thing humans had in common with seal-kin, then; gossip spread faster than illness.

"Not that I have heard," he said truthfully. "I suspect they won't. I was an idiot, pushing through the storm like that." Also true.

"You lived to learn from it, so that's the important thing," the woman said. "I'm Gert, and this is Sarah." The look she cast Sarah made it clear that there was an implied lesson for more than Dylan in that fact. He wondered what the two women were to each other; not mother and daughter, no, nor sisters. He didn't know enough about human society to understand, and for the first time, doubt struck. Being brought here…that implied that the female he had come to find was human. Everything he knew, everything he understood about females…would it apply to a human woman?

"There's no job waiting for you? No family?" the other man, Jonah, asked.

"No job," Dylan answered truthfully. "My family are fishermen, and they know I'll be back when I'm back."

Mike laughed. "Had enough of hauling nets and soaking in brine, did you? I spent a few summers working at a packing plant, and I swore the smell of fish would never get out of my pores. Money was good, though."

Money. He was going to need money. He should have thought of that before he let his hormones take over his brains, should have brought more to barter with than just his sister's anklet. Idiot. "I thought I might go into town and see if anyone needs a handyman. I'm pretty good with building and fixing."

"It's spring," Mike said thoughtfully. "Tourists'll be coming soon in hordes—sorry, folk," he said to the others, who merely laughed, not taking offense, "and everything needs to look pretty. You should be able to find some work pretty easily around here, if you're handy with a hammer." He eyed Dylan, as though judging how much of his sleek build was actually muscle. Dylan resisted the urge to stand up and try to present a larger silhouette, like a fur-cousin spoiling for a fight. At five-ten, he wasn't terribly impressive, until you looked more closely at his build. He wasn't sure he wanted anyone looking that closely at him.

"I haven't lost a thumb yet" was all he said.

"And if you've been a fisherman you're not afraid of hard work. Then you'll do." Mike nodded, coming to a decision. "I'll give you a list of folk you should talk to. Can't have a long-term boarder out of work now, can I?"

Everything was falling into place: the storm sending him here, of all the villages he might have come to, to the very beach where his mate waited. This man, giving him shelter and a reason to linger, to find her again.

Yes. He felt his impatience and restlessness stir again under his skin, and whispered to it the way he might a seal-pup, counseling patience. There would be time to swim in the great waters soon enough. Patience, for now.

And like a pup, his restlessness did not want to listen. Now, it insisted. Find her now. He could practically feel her in the air. She was close, close…all he had to do was find her.

After finishing her breakfast and coffee, Beth ran her assigned errand, strolling to the post office and standing on the line that had, wonders of wonders, actually formed. All of three people were in front of her, but in this town, before tourist season started, that was a notable wait.

Beth gave Ben's package over and asked for her own boxed mail, as well, when it was her turn.

While he went to fetch it, she leaned against the counter of the post office, her head turned just enough that she could watch people passing on the sidewalk beyond the plate-glass window of the storefront. She saw two friends walking past on the other side of the street going into the café, and realized that she hadn't seen either of them in weeks.

A dark-haired man walked past, on this side of the street, right in front of the post office, and Beth felt herself come to attention, somehow. A stranger with thick black hair down to his collar and a slender-hipped and yet sturdy build that caught her eye.

"No." It wasn't the stranger from the beach. It couldn't be. Or it could but even if it was, so what? Beth licked her lips, suddenly tasting salt and sea-musk on her skin, as though she had been out swimming, or washed her face with seawater. It reminded her of her dream, and her internal temperature rose several notches. The flush she felt inside was more annoying; what was she, sixteen again, to get so flustered at the sight of a good-looking stranger, dressed and ambulatory, or otherwise? And what the hell was she doing, walking out of the post office just to get a better look at him? Hello? Earth to Elizabeth?

Her feet weren't listening to her head, but she moved too slowly. By the time she went out the door, the bell jingling overhead, he was gone.

Beth stared down the street, wondering at herself, and the aching disappointment she felt. Was she that hard up, that a good-looking stranger got her juices running? Pitiful. But there was something about the figure, even glimpsed out of the corner of her eye… She had to fight the urge to run after him, ask him his name, anything to get him to notice her. She'd never felt any pull that hard, like the lure of fine chocolate at three in the morning, multiplied by ten.

"Oh, he was pretty, wasn't he?"

Beth flushed, and laughed at being caught—and by Sarah, of all people.

"Is the town starting a new beautification project?" she asked her old schoolmate and current Beautification Board member, who had also stopped on the sidewalk, apparently to watch the stranger walk by. Humor was better than admitting she had been caught in the act of goggling. "Because if so," she continued, "I gotta say, I approve."

"I wish," Sarah said. "But we'd have to raise taxes too much to afford that kind of pretty. You know who he is?"

"No…." Honesty forced her to add, "I think he's

our newest resident, the guy who washed up on shore."

"Really? Is he single?"

"You're not," Beth pointed out, fighting a surge of bitterness in her gut that surprised her. Was the eggroll suddenly disagreeing with her stomach?

"Oh. Right. Darn. And I was supposed to meet the hubby and the brats ten minutes ago. Don't be such a stranger!"

Beth promised, and then the postmaster waved from the counter, a large brown envelope in his hand. She went back in to pick up her packages, but her mind remained on the stranger in the street. Who was he? Why had such a quick glimpse of a stranger gotten her so worked up?

Maybe she had been running a fever, some kind of twenty-four-hour bug. That would explain everything, the weird twitches, the visual fluctuations, even the acid churning in her stomach. Maybe.

She walked out of the post office, her mail in hand, and looked across the street at the café where her friends had grabbed a table. She could see them inside, gesturing and laughing over their coffee. It was still early. Her bike was still locked up outside the diner. She should retrieve it and her safety helmet, go back to the house and get some work done. But even as she thought that, clutching her mail in one hand, Beth found herself torn between responsibility and a renewed restlessness.

Should, should… Suddenly, she didn't care so much about "should."

She tucked the packages into her bag and stepped off the curb, walking across the street to the café. She would take some time off, have a nice pot of tea with friends, instead of her usual solitary coffee. All in the name of taking care of her health, of course…

And absolutely nothing whatsoever to do with the fact that their window seat would be the perfect place to spot the stranger, if he walked by again.

Inland, across the bridge that connected the island to the mainland, in a small storefront office, a landline connected, and an old man picked up on the second ring. "Yes?" He didn't identify himself. Anyone who had this number was calling for only one reason, and names weren't required.

What they did wasn't illegal, technically. But only technically.

"You're certain?" he asked, pulling out a notepad and writing down the details. There was a plastic sheet under the page, preventing an impression being made on the sheet underneath. The technicality they worked under was best never tested in court.

The voice on the other end of the line was quite certain. The circumstances suggested, blood work confirmed, and he would like his bonus now, please.

"No sighting bonus until our team confirms," the man on the receiving end snapped, exasperated. Freelancers, bah. Every stray surfer, they tried to claim. "You have your stipend to tide you over, same as always. If you're as certain as you claim, then the bonus will be cut soon enough. We will be in touch."

He hung up the phone, and then picked it up again and dialed a single digit. There hadn't been a verified sighting here in almost two decades. But before then, this had been a major harvesting area. You didn't take chances, not with so much money involved.

"This is Station 22. I need to schedule a Hunt."

Chapter 4

The storm passed, but the restlessness remained. This morning, Beth didn't even pretend to be exercising, but instead found a large rock overlooking the ocean and climbed out onto it, letting her legs dangle off the edge exactly the way they warned teenagers about doing. A carafe of coffee beside her, and the remains of a cinnamon Danish on her lap, Beth stared out at the morning waves and tried to capture some of her usual serenity.

Now, that serenity felt more like death, and the camera on the opposite side of her, the object that usually gave her context for her moods, remained capped and unused.

She had dreamed again last night. Not an erotic

dream this time, but a sad one. A dream of loss, and longing, and lose-lose scenarios. On waking, the details had fled. But as she stared into the gray-blue of the Atlantic, the memory stirred…

His daughter was crying.…

In the dream, it was a lovely summer's morning, the sun barely breaking over the rooftops of the village. A man stood in the surf, the cold blue-green Atlantic waters washing about his ankles, the gritty wet sand moving below his bare feet, a fish braver or more foolish than the rest of its school nibbling curiously at the rough fabric of his trousers. The rest of his clothing he had left, clean and neatly folded, on the bed in the cottage. When his son, his Isaac, grew to a man's height, he could wear them.

Or they could be passed on, still fashionable, if Sarah took another husband.

The thought should not be a hook in his gut, so surprisingly sharp and painful. Was he then so easily replaced? He had never meant to linger so long, never meant to make a life here, never meant to create children…Isaac and baby Ruth. His children, his and Sarah's.

Bright-eyed Sarah. Fearless Sarah, who faced down storms and sickness with such calm courage and practical sure-handedness. Who had found him wracked up in the rocks after a bad storm four years before and taken him in, nursed him to health, and asked no questions when he slipped out of her bed and down to the sea—and asked no questions when he came back, wrapping sea-damp arms around her, kissing away her tears with salt-streaked lips. Who ignored the tsking of the village women to bear his children, sell his daily catch of fish in the market: who had every reason to believe that she would grow old with him at her side.

The thought pained him, that he would disappoint her so. And yet...

Come home, the sea whispered to him, as it had for a week or more, now, until he could no longer resist. *It is time to come home.*

He had loved Sarah, their family, as well as he could, as much and as long as a mortal could be loved by one such as he. Sarah knew that. They had their season, and more. It was time, past time for him to go. That was how all stories such as theirs ended.

Come home.

He missed his colony, the sounds of his kin. And yet...

"I can't." He didn't know who he was speaking to, what he was denying. His feet moved him deeper into the water, even as his heart tied him to the land.

His brave Sarah, crying.

His daughter was crying.

Come home.

The water always takes back its own.

He took another step, and stopped.

"Not this time. Tethys, forgive me, not this time."

A stillness in the waves, the water chilling against his skin, urging him in.

"I…cannot. My home is here now."

The stillness broke, the sea's voice replaced by another. *There is a price for what you ask….*

"Anything. For them…for them anything I will pay."

The voice went on as though it had not heard him. *There is a price…that all must pay. Forever.*

The dream, the memory faded and disappeared, yet *forever* echoed in Beth's ears, a sense of inexplicable loss settling in her soul, and a single salty tear escaped, unnoticed, from the corner of her eye as she stared out into the hypnotic flow of the ocean.

Dylan wanted to swear. Four days. Four days since he had given in to the itch, left the safety of his home and swum into human lands, the totally human world. This small village was close enough to his own home that he could adapt, but the bits and pieces he caught, in the ads and conversations around him, were overwhelming.

Still, the basics were always the same. Food, shelter and clothing came first. Dylan pushed his selections across the counter, and watched as the clerk totaled the cost of each into a sum. He had enough to cover it, but the fold of bills in his pocket was not as thick as it had been only a few days before. Still, he needed the new underwear and socks, as well as the two long-sleeved pullover shirts, and a pair of cotton pants the same faded green as the knapsack he had picked out to hold it all.

Army surplus, the clerk had said when he picked it up, and that triggered another set of memories in Dylan's head. Men, and things exploding into the water. Men swimming, being pulled to land. Some of them going away, after, and some of them staying. His great-grandfather had been one of those men pulled to safety by his great-grandmother, according to family stories, Dylan remembered now. A human sailor: one of the ones who stayed. That was the source of the memories, then.

He welcomed the memories, and the information they brought; his people were seal-kin, after all, not seals. This confusing land was as much his legacy as the ocean and wind, for all that he had never explored it much before now.

He paid the final charge and shoved everything into the knapsack, adjusting the straps to fit comfortably over his shoulder. "Thanks," he said to the clerk, who paused in shutting the register's drawer to smile in return. "No problem. Have a good day, mister."

Leaving the store, Dylan paused in front of another storefront window, drawn by something in the display. Bright sticks of color, each the size of one of his fingers, wrapped in paper and just begging to be picked up and drawn across a surface. Like the chalks he used at home, but softer, creamier. It was only a hobby, his drawing, but he missed it.

He mentally counted how much cash he had left from the anklet, after buying clothing and paying for the room, then looked at the chalks again. Not enough. Not if he didn't find work soon. Dylan

didn't want to rely on Dr. Alden's charity, but he
didn't know, anymore, how long finding Her would
take, and… And he could almost feel the chalks
under his fingers, could almost see the swaths of
color they would leave behind.

It was stupid. He was here to find his mate, and
then go home. That was what drove him. The sense
of urgency moved within him, reminding him that
he didn't have forever. He had enough paints and
brushes at home, and he would be back with them
soon enough, once his mission was done.

And yet, suddenly he found himself inside the
store, buying the sticks, and a pad of thick white
paper, and a fat brush with soft bristles, to smooth
the colors together in ways he could already en-
vision in his mind. The thought made him smile.

"Nice choice. You planning to do some sketching, while you're here?" The woman standing next
to him in line barely came up to his shoulder, with
bright blue eyes and white hair sleeked back into a
long, sophisticated-looking braid.

"I might." He hadn't planned to, but while they
didn't soothe the restlessness in his blood any, the
feel of the sticks—Cray-Pas, they were called on
the box—made the tightness in his shoulders relax
a little. Drawing always helped him think, and he
needed to think, and to plan. He was already realizing that this village was larger than he had thought
at first, with more people coming in and out. How
was he to find his mate? Simply wandering around
sniffing for her had seemed a good idea that first

morning, but it wasn't going to be that easy, he knew already. Standing in the green square outside and bellowing his claim might work for the old bulls, but he couldn't quite see that working for a female, human or seal-kin.

The woman made a noise through her nose, like a laugh but not quite, and Dylan looked curiously at her. Something about the way she looked at him...

She avoided his gaze and moved off, apparently abandoning in a small red basket the assortment of brushes that she had planned to buy.

Strange. Humans were very, very strange.

He paid for the supplies with his precious cash and left the store, trying to decide if he could fit the white plastic bag of supplies in his knapsack along with the clothing, or if the shoving required would crease the pad. Finally he decided that he couldn't, and resigned himself to carrying the bag in his hand.

"Hey. You. Dylan, right?"

He turned slowly, still not comfortable with the sound of the name he had given himself, even though his race-memory said it meant "of the sea" and should therefore fit him as well as any. "Yes?"

The man who had hailed him was tall and skinny, sun-browned skin stretched tight over bones. "Thought so. You move like a local but you don't look like one. Don't sound like one, neither. Anyway, Mike said you were handy with a tool kit?"

Mike was the innkeeper, Mike Brandt.

"Yes."

"Excellent. You need work and I've some things need fixin'. Shames me to say it but I never got the hang of hammer and nails. And I'm too cheap to pay a professional to do it, and here you come along like it was all planned to be. Oh, I'm Nathan," he added, naming himself almost as an afterthought, part of the running flow of words. "Come on, come on, I'll show you what I need done, and we can argue over how little I'm going to pay you. I'm cheap—cheap and poor. But there's lunch involved. I can't hammer but I damn well can cook."

Dylan juggled the bag and knapsack to more comfortable positions for carrying, and followed Nathan down the street, as helpless in the talking man's wake as a newborn seal pup in an undertow.

He hated that feeling as he had never hated anything in his life, hated being dependent on others, hated not being able to simply go through the town until he found Her, swept Her up in his arms and took Her away with him.

That thought made him shake his head in self-disgust. He might be new at this wooing thing, but he wasn't an idiot. That would get him slapped, if not worse, by even the most forgiving of seal-kin women. No reason to think human women would be any different.

He had to find her, first, and then figure out the best way to approach her. Find out what she was like, what she liked. Then he could woo her properly.

Home, he would have brought her a particularly tasty, fresh-caught fish or colorful deep-sea shells, made fragrant reed baskets or whimsical sand structures.... Maybe she liked paper drawings? Or needed something rebuilt?

Seal bulls had it easier. But they also had to go through it every season, searching through the available females of the colony.

The one thing Dylan knew was that he had to be careful, out among humans. That lesson was taught early on, along with the dangers of sharks, barracudas and riptides. It wasn't all swimming and seducing, the way the songs claimed. There were more dangers on land than on sea. Humans hated what was different—hated, and envied it. And all too often, killed it.

So he needed to be careful. Careful, but not so careful he wasted any more time, and risked losing her scent.

While he was trying to figure out how to ask what he wanted, they arrived at their destination: a storefront with "Eat Here. You Won't Regret It" in red lights, under a larger wooden sign proclaiming the space a diner named Apollo's.

"After you," Nathan said, holding open the glass door. There was no jingle of bells or chimes overhead, unlike most of the other stores Dylan had gone into, but the wall of sound was a pleasant unbroken hum, even as the people seated inside paused to see who had come in before going back to their lunch.

"Over here," Nathan said, bringing Dylan with him to the counter. Dylan took one look and winced, all other thoughts going out of his head.

Nathan hadn't been kidding when he said that he wasn't handy with tools. The mess he had made out of something as simple as fixing the hinges on the counter made Dylan flinch, and before he had time to think about what he might charge, the hatch was removed, the hinges unscrewed, and he was ordering Nathan to go find him some sandpaper, wood oil and rust remover, as well as a screwdriver and a pair of pliers.

Nathan got all of those things, plus a large Coke, which he set on the counter next to Dylan, and watched the younger man start sanding down the area around the hinges, removing the splintered areas. "You really do know what you're doing."

"Mmm." Dylan wasn't much for talking, but Nathan clearly was. The human leaned against the other side of the counter and watched him work, when he wasn't shouting orders to the rest of the staff. The café, Apollo's, seemed to cater mostly to old men and teenagers, even though there were framed watercolors of children on the wall, and soft music playing in the background.

Nathan shook his head, either impressed at Dylan's skill, or astonished at his silence while working. "Tell you what, fix this, and install the window screens so that's done before anyone starts yelling at me to open windows and let fresh air in, and I'll pay you a hundred dollars, cash, and throw lunch in, like I promised. And then we can talk about what else I'm going to need done, because Lord knows, there's work that needs capable hands."

Money always made his head hurt, which was why he mostly stayed close to home when he could, but it was essential to getting by in human society. A hundred wouldn't go far, even with that, but he shouldn't have to stay longer than a week or two, and if he ran out of cash he could always go fishing for his meals. He was already missing the feel of the waves over his shoulders, the buoyancy of the ocean around him. Land was so…heavy.

"Deal?" Nathan asked.

"Deal."

They shook on it, and Dylan went back to work, smoothing the splintered wood to his satisfaction, then reapplying the newly greased hinges and attaching the hatch to it. The work engrossed him, soothed him at least temporarily, and he tuned out everything else and let his hands take over.

Slipping out to the other side of the counter to test how it lifted and lowered, he backed up a step, and collided with a warm, soft body.

His own body tensed, even as he whipped around, his hands reaching up and out to hold on to his discovery. Her. After days of searching, without result, the moment he relaxed and didn't think about it for five minutes, it was *Her*.

"Oh. Hi. Sorry about that."

Her voice wasn't as soft or as sweet as he remembered. Her sweat didn't have quite the same salty musk he thought he had tasted the first time she touched him, that storm-wracked night on the beach. But he would know her anywhere, in a

room of a hundred other humans. In a pitch-black
room at midnight, he would know her, just from
the way his pulse raced, and he felt himself grow
hard at her presence.

She backed away, and he stared. He couldn't
help it. She was slender, but well-muscled, almost
matching him perfectly in height. Her skin was sun-
flushed cream, her eyes warm brown with flecks of
pale green, like ocean foam, and her hair, cut short
and ruffled like a gull's pinfeathers, was the same
silky black as his own.

His heart raced, his pulse leaping again in sudden
realization. Human, yes. Undoubtedly human. But
not *entirely* human. Those eyes, that hair—seal-kin
blood had touched her family, somewhere, somehow. She was seal-kin!

The relief he felt washed over him and left him
wobbly-kneed and breathless. It all made sense
now. His instincts hadn't misled him, or sent him
on an impossible quest for a mate who would never
understand or be happy with his kind. Now he knew
what to do.

Beth almost dropped the mail she had been sorting while she waited for her lunch order to be rung
up when the guy she had bumped in to turned
around and grabbed her. First there was shock at
being manhandled like that, and then she looked up
into his face and realized that it was the man from
the street—the man from the beach.

He was as good-looking as she'd thought, from that

brief glimpse, and the hold he had on her was strong without being harsh or intimidating. She should have taken offense, but all she could do was stare.

His dark brown eyes went even rounder, staring at her as well, and his narrow-lipped mouth opened, as though in shock. She resisted the urge to wipe at her face, certain she had a smudge or something on the tip of her nose, he was looking so intently at her face.

"You." He wasn't angry, or surprised, or anything else that she might have expected. In fact, he sounded…satisfied? Smug, even. A low voice: toffee-flavored and definitely not a local accent, even in that one word. British? No, with more of a burr to it—Scottish? Faint, but it was there.

He blinked, annoyingly long dark lashes sweeping down and up again, and then those eyes looked right into her, like she had no secrets, no surprises from him, like she belonged with him, to him, and nowhere else ever again.

A sudden rush went through her body, like being sparked with static electricity, only a hundred times stronger. Beth beat down the wild flutter in her stomach and got a firmer grip on her mail, even as the guy down at the other end of the counter called out her order.

"Sorry," she said again, extricating herself from his grip—he let go, the moment she resisted, she noted—and backing away. "So sorry, my mistake, gotta go."

Her pulse beat so strongly in her throat she

could feel it. She was running away. Why was she running away? The guy hadn't done anything, in fact, he'd been polite and soft-spoken, if a little obvious in his interest.

Because, she realized, she was scared. Terrified. Turned on, and scared out of her mind by it.

By him. By the rush that had turned her knees into overcooked noodles.

What the hell was going on? She didn't react this way. Ever. Not to anyone.

She accepted her club sandwich and cream soda from the clerk, and risked looking over her shoulder, driven by some desire she didn't quite understand.

He was leaning against the counter, hands shoved into the pockets of his pants, watching her. His face was serious, his eyes intent on her. Way too intent.

Beth looked away first, blushing. She wasn't used to men looking at her like that, any more than she was used to reacting so strongly to a stranger. It was…disturbing.

"You okay, hon?" The clerk looked at her as if she thought Beth was about to pass out. Maybe she was. Why else did she feel all sweaty and faint, like she'd just done a mile run on an empty tank?

"Yeah. Just need to put some food in me," she said with a smile, taking her change and shoving it into her pocket. She wanted to flee the café entirely, but she had gotten her meal for here, and there was no graceful way to pack it to go now.

So she moved to a table as far away from the counter as she could get, putting several groups between her and the stranger she knew was still staring at her. The food was suddenly unappetizing, but she forced it down anyway, one bite at a time, washing it down with her iced tea methodically, never looking away from what she was doing.

"Who was that?" Dylan asked Nathan, still trying to remember how to breathe.

"The poor girl you almost sent running for the hills?" Nathan was leaning back, arms crossed over his chest, his face stern but his eyes alight with laughter.

"Yes. Her." Dylan had no sense of humor at that moment. She was there, she saw him! Touched him! And she ran. Why? Who was she? Other than seal-kin, and how, here? How could they not know? How had the community lost track of her, and were there others?

"That's Beth Havelock. Nice girl. Grew up here. Hell, her family's almost one of the founders, they go back so far. Sailing family. Been a Havelock in Seastone since, oh, roundabouts mid-1800s or so. Maybe even earlier.

"She's also dating a local boy, name of Jake. You might want to reconsider your interest—they've been together a long time, even if Beth hasn't shown much thought to white dresses and bouquets as of yet. With women, who can tell?"

Dylan had stopped paying attention to Nathan's

chatter. A family here for generations, descendant from a retired sailor…the pieces began to slip together now.

Clearly, he wasn't the only seal-kin to come west for a mate. But why had they cut themselves off from the colony? Why had none of them ever come back to find a mate for themselves? That was more than unusual, it was unheard-of. Seal-kin found seal-kin, lived in a colony. It just…was the way it was.

No matter. She was here. He had found her. It was only a matter of the wooing, now, and he could take her home, back where she belonged.

But for the first time a shadow of real doubt moved in him. How did you woo someone who ran away from you? She wasn't playing coy, either; he had scared her, somehow. And she was seeing someone else?

Dylan took a deep breath and forced himself to look away from his mate—from Beth—and went back to work with the sandpaper. "How serious are they, her and that…other guy?"

Nathan stared at him, then shook his head, all joking gone. "Ah. That way, is it? All right, I may regret this, but what the hell. I never did think they were a good match, Beth and that boy, and we always need a good handyman in town." He leaned forward onto the counter, as though imparting some deep and terrible secret. "First thing is, play it cool. You already went in with the blunt, caveman routine, and that didn't work so well, did it? Beth's a local girl, and she appreciates a little context, a little familiarity—but the appeal of something or some*one* new's gonna get her, too. You gotta work 'em both. Show her you can fit into her world, but intrigue her with what you know, what you've seen. Make her wonder what she could learn from you, that's the trick."

Dylan leaned in, and paid attention.

In Apollo's, a woman sitting alone at a booth near the back paid her bill, leaving a respectable but not overly generous tip, and left the diner, pausing to let a man and his daughter walk in, the little girl's pigtails swinging in anticipation of an egg cream. She went out to the sidewalk, down several store-fronts, and withdrew her cell phone. The woman was of moderate height and weight, a long white braid coiled stylishly on the back of her head. She was dressed well but unobtrusively so; the sort to rate a passing glance from the locals, but no more. Totally ordinary. Totally harmless. She pressed a button on speed dial, and waited.

"Report's confirmed, two encounters and we have a lock." Her voice was as unobtrusive as her appearance, unless you were paying close attention to the steel underlying the lack of a noticeable regional accent.

The voice on the other end of the connection was male, and equally steely. "You're sure?"

She pursed her lips, staring at some invisible point in the shop's display window. "How long have I been doing this?"

"Not as long as I have. You need to be sure."

He was the boss. Obligingly, she recited the data. "He landed on the beach, naked as the day he was born—except a silver-and-black pearl bit of jewelry, which he then sold to pay his way. He is using the name Dylan Meridith, which has been recorded before in the Hunt Records. And he's got the Look."

Any one of those things would have been interesting. Two might have been coincidence. Three or more, and she had justification for making this phone call. The initial outlier might have run tests, but only a Hunter was trained to make the final determination.

"All right." It took experience to hear the pleasure in her boss's voice. "I'll send the rest of the team in."

"You don't need—"

He cut her off. "You did a good job. If it pans out, nobody's going to push you out of the reckoning. But the deal doesn't get done single-handed, you should know that."

She did. She just wanted assurance that she would be the lead on this. The lead took the largest share of the profit.

"Keep an eye on him. We'll be in touch."

She closed her mobile phone with a click, then turned and walked down the street, away from the store, heading to her car. She was staying in the next town over, to prevent her face from becoming too familiar. If this panned out, and the selkie was taken? She smiled, a bright, pleased smile that made her entire face light up. If this panned out, she was on her way to bigger and better things, for sure.

All it took was one lock and acquisition, after all, and a woman was set, financially. Demand was always high, and supply low, and that was good news for a Hunter.

Chapter 5

Day Seven. A full week of playing by Nathan's advice. The need to do more, to claim his mate and take her, was almost unbearable, driving him out of bed early with the restlessness and hunger.

Dylan slipped off his canvas sneakers and dug his bare toes into the sand the moment he stepped off the path and onto the beach. The morning was promising to be a fine one, the sun so low on the horizon it was barely a glimmer on the water, the smell of the spray sweet and bitter on his tongue. The feel of the cool wet sand under his bare feet as he walked was as familiar as his mother's voice, and just as soothing. The tide was low, and the usual debris of stranded crabs and shellfish were scattered for the gulls to pick at, warning others with out-stretched wings to stay away.

How many mornings in previous years had he spent, just so, walking along shorelines like this one?

Those mornings, he had been content. Alone or with company, it had not mattered. Now, the itch to be part of another was driving him insane, every moment except when he was here, near the sea-water. He had named his nonexistent boat *Daughter of the Sea,* but he was the child of Tethys in truth, never happy out of reach of her embrace.

But the touch of his mate's hand…it lured him onto the land, and there it would stay, until he could claim her, once and for all.

It was just…taking a while.

"Taking implies action," he told a gull, who looked deeply unimpressed. "I've not had the chance to do anything yet. Nothing except talk and talk and talk to everyone *but* her!" He knew, just seeing her, scenting her. How could she not? How could she deny it, hide from him the way she had been doing?

Humans were strange. But she was more than human…. How did the knowledge elude her? How could she not know who he was, what he was to her?

Love is never easy, he could hear his mother saying, laughing kindly. *Do not despair, my son.*

The gull cawed once, then spread his wings and flew away, as though to mock his own lack of movement.

"Arrrgh!" he called to the gull, envying it the freedom to just *go* like that.

"Hey-ya, Dylan." A man's voice came from a low folding beach chair set firmly in the morning-damp sand, a few yards from the water's edge.

"Morning, Dylan." Another voice, this one rougher, with longer years' exposure to salt, sea and smoke, rising from a similar folding chair set next to the first. Fishing poles protruded from the packed sand on either side of the chairs, the line stretched out into the water, and a red bucket was placed between them to hold whatever they might catch.

Josh and Ned: father and son, out every morning before dawn to cast their lures and drink coffee and smoke foul-scented cigars. Dylan had seen them out here every morning all week, even when it was raining hard enough to send sane people running for cover. He suspected they came out as much to smoke the cigars as actually fish.

"Anything biting?" He asked every morning, and every morning the answer was the same. This morning, though, Ned pulled a still-live fish from the red bucket, holding it properly by the gills. "Cod're frisky this morning."

"Nice. Good eating." His mouth was watering, actually. The crisp clean taste of the flesh, served with fresh-baked bread, and a side of seaweed or salted rice…

Seal-kin food, not human. Somehow, the oatmeal, bacon and eggs waiting for him back at the

B and B didn't appeal as much as it had when he got up and smelled it cooking. But it was included in the cost, so that was what he would have, along with the usual smoked fish offerings. Maybe Nathan would make him fresh fish for lunch.

He left the two fishermen to their cigars and fishing lines and headed farther on down the empty stretch of beach. It was barely that, just a strip of sand below low dunes, facing out into the ocean. Shingle houses with huge plate-glass windows looked out over the bluff onto the waterfront, but the sand itself was practically invisible until you were on it. He had stumbled on it purely by accident, walking aimlessly his first day, not quite sure what to do with himself. It had become a ritual of sorts, since then, to come and watch the sun rise, and do a little sketching, to settle his thoughts and plan his day.

He had been working at the diner for three days now, and he had managed to completely redo the broken counter hinge, refinish the counter around it so that the repair couldn't be seen and fix half a dozen cabinets in the kitchen so that the doors swung easily and the shelves didn't sag. He had also met at least half of the town's population—everyone seemed to come into Apollo's for lunch, dinner or coffee in between.

Everyone except Beth Havelock. Nathan said she usually came in once or twice a week, when she needed a break from work, but it wasn't always and it wasn't regular.

And, Dylan suspected, it wouldn't be while he

was still working there. She was definitely hiding from him.

"Handled that one with all the finesse of a flounder," he muttered, finding a spare bit of beach and dropping his knapsack on the sand. She had been there, right in front of him. Aware of him, he would trade his skin on that. If he hadn't been so…stupid, so impulsive, and scared her away like a clumsy bull…

Well. Nothing to be done now except fix it, as his mother would say.

He knelt down and took out the pad of paper, his Cray-Pas and a small assortment of wooden dowels. A few confident movements, and the dowels turned into a short easel just large enough to hold the sketch pad at a comfortable height for him to work on when seated cross-legged on the sand.

No, Beth Havelock wasn't coming to him. So he was going to have to go to her. He had met a woman, Joyce was her name. Rounded like a dolphin and almost as cheerful. She was a friend of Beth's, Nathan said. If he couldn't approach his mate directly, she might be the way to go. Cute, in a land-dweller sort of way—there were very few blondes among his people. More redheads, interestingly enough. Too many Celtic sailors, his grandfather used to say while rubbing his own ginger-graying hair, falling for dark-eyed selkie women.

Maybe Joyce wouldn't mind playing go-between and coaxing Beth somewhere so he could actually approach her, try to woo her properly?

A go-between. Yes. He knew now who her particular friends were, the woman Joyce, and the couple who ran the diner on the edge of town. If he could win them over, convince them he was genuinely interested in Beth—and he was—then maybe they would help him.

The only squall might be the boyfriend. He had come in a few times, and Nathan had pointed him out. Once by himself, twice with another woman. No, the boyfriend wasn't a problem. He would have sensed it, if his mate was spending any time with that man, if she had been intimate with him....

The thought, the faintest shadow of another man touching his mate, and his gut clenched in near-agony, a red sheen of rage. *No.* He forced himself to calm down. He was not a bull seal, to become mindlessly violent with need. He was seal-kin, and he would be patient.

The easel set up, he opened the sketch pad and let a different part of his brain take over. He had been right; the colored sticks did flow smoothly, the connection between eye and hand almost instantaneous.

He would arrange things so that she had no choice but to come to him. If he asked Joyce, used her romantic nature…used the couple's desire to see their friend happy…

It was trickier than he liked, trickier than his nature enjoyed. If it worked, he would apologize over and over again, until she relented and forgave him.

Between his thoughts and the soothing act of

sketching, before he knew it the sun had risen well into the sky, and he had filled four sheets with seascapes that he was almost satisfied with. Almost, but not quite. There was something missing from the horizon, some element that should have been there and wasn't. Waves, sky, distant passing ships, the occasional flipper of dolphins or the silvery splash of a school of fish... All there, and yet something lacked.

He shook his head, unable to put a finger on it. His stomach rumbled, and he noted that Ned and Josh had already packed up and headed home for their own breakfast. He carefully placed onionskin over the drawings, closed the pad and placed the sticks and pad back into his knapsack. Brushing dry sand off of his butt and pant legs, Dylan froze, some warning system going off in the back of his brain.

Danger. Danger. Be still, go low.

There was nowhere to go low, on the beach, but he stayed on his knees, barely breathing, waiting for the dark shadow of danger to slide by.

Nothing. No movement. No threat. But his instincts were screaming at him that something was wrong, something was trouble. Someone—a predator—was watching him.

Nothing moved. Nothing attacked.

He forced himself to stand up, standing tall against the horizon, a perfect target.

Nothing happened.

Taking a deep breath, Dylan picked up his knapsack and forced himself to walk normally down the beach, fighting the urge to run every step of the way until he came to the end of the deserted strip of beach, within view of the nearest homes along the road. In that moment, the feeling of danger disappeared, and he was alone once again.

"Come on. You've been mewed up here all week, and the weather is gorgeous, and pretty soon the tourists will show up and it will be impossible to go anywhere without tripping over them."

Beth kept her back to her friend, trying to focus on the negative she had on the light-box in front of her. Joyce was exaggerating, anyway. Tourists came here, but mainly the ones who wanted a quiet, relaxing getaway, the honeymooners or the older adults. It never got as bad as some of the more picturesque towns or, God help them, Cape Cod.

Although, the weather had been lovely, as though apologizing for the damage the storm had done: bright blue skies and clear sunlight, with constant light breezes off the water keeping the air cool and comfortable. Perfect spring weather, the kind that was rare on the New England coast, and you were supposed to appreciate when it came by.

She hadn't even been out for her run this morning. Dreams had kept her tossing and turning all night, and when she woke up the last thing she had wanted to do was get up and sweat.

Her dreams—again erotic, if only dimly remembered—had her sweating enough. The voice of a man, calling to her, and the sound of waves mixing with his voice, and over it all that taste of sea-spray and salt water on her tongue, and rising from her skin when she finally awoke...

"Beeeeeeetttttth. Come on. And don't tell me you're working. You were complaining two weeks ago that work was slow and you were thinking about taking a vacation! Come on, you're turning into a dried-up, no-fun prune!"

Beth swiveled around in her work chair and stared at her friend. Joyce had been her best friend in grade school. They had sworn to be best friends forever in fifth grade, and even when different interests took them in opposite directions, the friendship remained.

Beth was starting to reconsider that, right about now.

Joyce was sprawled on the old blue velvet love seat in Beth's office, her tailored pinstripe pantsuit a marked contrast to Beth's jeans and long-sleeved polo. High-heeled shoes had been kicked off and lay discarded on the floor, and she was rubbing the instep of one foot with the steady moves of someone whose feet always hurt.

Joyce Caylor had gotten her MBA right after college, and should have been off somewhere learning to run the world. Instead, she had come home after her mom's heart attack, and was learning to run her parents' bait and tackle with her dad. She still dressed like a benevolent Wall Street tyrant, though, and nobody doubted that within ten years the one successful store would become a chain of successful sport fishing supply stores, probably with guides-for-hire and a line of associated charter boats.

You didn't say no to Joyce, not without a damn good reason and the strength to stand your ground. Beth had the strength, but her reasons…

I got freaked by a good-looking guy looking like he wanted to put me up against the wall and screw me until we both passed out is probably not going to go over as a good reason, she thought wryly. Even if it was the truth, and no more or less than what Joyce would expect from her more cautious friend.

As though scenting surrender in the air, her best friend's green eyes brightened. "Come on. I'll buy lunch." Joyce swung her legs over the side of the love seat and sat up straight. "And we can go somewhere other than Apollo's, if you're that freaked out over one good-looking guy."

Beth's mouth opened to deny it, but nothing came out, making her look and feel like a fish.

Damn old, lifelong best friends, anyway.

"All right?" Joyce was practically purring with satisfaction.

"All right," she agreed, sliding the negatives she had been working with into a dust-free cover and turning the light-box off. Because Joyce, as usual, was right on the money. Beth *was* bored, she *was* tired of the same four walls and she *was* changing her schedule because of one stranger in town, which was…ridiculous. "You're buying lunch, and I'm picking the place." Somewhere far away from Apollo's, in feel if not in distance.

Ten minutes later they were piling out of Joyce's lime-green VW Bug in front of Ben and Glory's diner, laughing at some inane joke that didn't even make sense to them but was hysterically funny anyway if you had been in the car with the two of them. Beth walked in the door first, and then stopped dead, making Joyce run hard into her.

"Ow! What's the deal, brick wall?"

The deal was sitting at the front table, leaning back against the leatherette banquette like he owned the place.

So much for her choosing somewhere safe. Honestly. Didn't the man have work to do? Wasn't he supposed to be at Apollo's, not slutting around in other restaurants?

She knew she was being irrational and squelched her annoyance. It was a free country, and he could go wherever he wanted. Nobody was forcing them to interact, after all. He hadn't done anything objectionable, really. A touch, a look…

Look like he wanted to devour her, yeah. Touch her with fingers that burned. And asking about her, endlessly, since that moment, until he knew everything about her. It was a small town, off-season, and he was new blood. Handsome new blood, with a touch of mystery. It would take stronger folk than her neighbors to resist that. She couldn't really blame them.

But oh, how she resented being part of it! Especially since she knew nothing at all about *him*.

Ben was at the table with him, looking intently

at a bunch of sheets of paper on the table, while Gena, who was another old schoolmate, now an architect, hovered by his shoulder. Gena looked up and saw Beth and waved, then pointed to the counter where…oh, joy, Jake was waiting for his coffee. This just wasn't her day, was it?

"I should have stayed in the office," she muttered, and headed for Jake before he could turn and see her. Might as well deal with this right away.

"Hey, stranger." She didn't mean to startle him, but the way he jumped when she came up next to him suggested that his brain was somewhere else. "Sorry."

"No, no, my fault." He grabbed a few napkins and blotted at the spill of coffee. "Was thinking when I should have been looking. Guy-brain, we only manage one thing at a time."

It was a long-standing joke between them; while most people could and would multitask, they were both happier when faced with a single task they could devote everything to, finish it and then move on. Guy-brain, Jake claimed.

Beth used to take it as a compliment. Now, it annoyed her. Was that how he saw her—as another one of the guys?

Maybe she was. Maybe that was the problem.

"You been busy?" He hadn't called her again to reschedule dinner. She hadn't called him, either. He was kind enough—or clueless enough—not to point that out.

"Nine-tailed cat, room full of rocking chairs," he

agreed. "Added three summer houses to my rotation, Gena's clients. She recommended me." A slight hesitation, before he continued. "She's been sending a lot of work my way."

"Oh."

She waited for even a hint of jealousy, a sour curdling in her stomach at the thought of him spending time with the admittedly lovely and perfectly single Gena. Nothing. Not even a twinge. In fact, she felt…relief.

"Hey, Miss Elizabeth! Over here!"

Ben's summons saved her from having to respond one way or the other to Jake's news, and she gave her soon-to-be-ex-for-good boyfriend a faint smile before going over to the table. From one unwanted encounter to an even less-wanted encounter: He was there.

She had seen him in town, of course. Across the street, working in the café, or down on the beach in the morning, knapsack in hand. She had changed her exercise routine to avoid the shoreline, trying to stay away from him. In the end, it was all pointless. Here he was. Here she was.

Beth Havelock had never been a quitter, damn it. Sometimes it just…took her a while to work up to the battle.

Despite that, the closer she got to where Ben and…He sat, the more she wanted to run. Her body felt too warm, like she had been sitting in the summer sun for hours without protection, and her eyes itched like she had sudden-onset allergies.

Lewd images tried to elbow their way into her brain, slinky, sweaty images of limbs tangled, bodies bracing, merging, rising and falling in a wave....

"Beth, have you met Dylan?"

Bastard. Ben knew damn well she had met him. The entire town knew she had met him. She hoped that her face wasn't as flushed as it felt.

"We ran in to each other in the café," he said, and the laughter in his voice tempted her just enough that she looked at him. Sideways, briefly, but it was enough. Too much. His face was turned up to her and their gazes crossed and locked.

Her breath stopped and the fluttery panicked feeling started again in her chest. Those eyes...she remembered those eyes from her dreams. Those eyes, and those hands, stroking her skin, so tenderly, but with possession in them, too. Her name on his lips, his breath in her ear, the feel of water lapping at them, blood-warm and salty.

Her elbows—her *elbows!*—felt weak, and her knees wobbled, and she tasted blood, salt and spray on her lips, until she licked them just to make sure it wasn't real, and she had the horrible feeling that she whimpered.

Dylan made a noise, a low whisper of something she wasn't sure he even knew he was saying, low enough that the only way she knew he had said something was that she saw his lips move.

Beth looked away quickly, back to Ben's face, before she humiliated herself further.

"He's quite the artist," Ben was saying, indicating the drawings spread out on the table in front of him. "I don't know why he's bothering with the handyman gig—he should be hawking these at crafts fairs and galleries. Not that I know anything about art, but I bet these would sell. Don't you have artist friends, on the mainland, who could give us an opinion?"

"That's really not needful," Dylan said hastily, reaching out to reclaim the drawings, his arms over the sheets as though to protect them from being seen. "They're just scribbles."

Beth hadn't wanted to take a look at all, hadn't wanted to be anywhere near the man who made her feel so off-kilter. But to be rebuffed that way, her opinion unwanted, her influence dismissed…that stung as much as his physical presence appealed, and her wobbly knees locked even as her spine stiffened.

"If it's not needful, then I won't waste either of our time," she said, her voice as stiff as her back. Ben started to say something, and she looked at him, her gaze daring him to make even one sound.

He didn't.

She nodded to him, ignoring the other man at the table as best she could with every nerve ending still madly aware of him, his arms still curved over his drawings, his body half-turned to her. The body language was just as confusing as her own physical reaction, and she fled to the table Joyce had gotten them, her appetite completely gone but damned if she would be driven out of one more place by that… Idiot.

And it was only a faint flicker of weakness that

made her replay, over and over again, that involuntary word, the movement of his lips, breathing out a single word: *beloved*.

"Well," she didn't hear Ben say. "That went well, don't you think?"

And she didn't see Dylan put his face down on the table, on top of his drawings, and beat his forehead, gently, against the laminate. "I'm doomed."

"Yah," Ben agreed sadly, trying to pull the drawings away before they were smudged. "I'm afeared you are."

Chapter 6

Beth stared at the screen in exasperation. Two weeks, ever since just before the storm, she had been twitchy, distracted and generally short-tempered. And now she had just ruined three hours of hard work with one thoughtless keystroke.

It was all His fault. She was blaming everything on Him, from the delightful weather she wasn't getting to enjoy to the tension in her own skin, to the fact that she had run out of orange juice and had to go into town if she wanted any, and going to town meant she might run in to Him—or worse, someone who wanted to sing His praises into her I-don't-care ears.

She knew damn well that she was overreacting,

and she didn't care. Maybe everyone in town wasn't actually behaving like Yenta, the matchmaker from *Fiddler on the Roof,* but it sure felt like it. The more they pushed him, the more she wanted to push him away. Ben's and Glory's comments came back to her—that she would do things on her own schedule.

"Damn right," she agreed. Nice to know that they, at least, understood her. Also, hello? Still in a relationship. Sort of.

The studio phone rang, and she thought about picking it up but decided against it. Someone might be calling to offer her a million-dollar contract, and she would be snippy with them, at this rate.

"You've reached the Havelock Agency. Please leave your name, number, and a brief message, and we will return your call as soon as possible. Thank you for your interest, and we hope you have a good day."

A gentle chime, and the message ended.

"Beth? I know you're there, Beth." Joyce. Again. "I'm sitting here looking out the window and I can see that the light is on in your studio. Pick up the phone. Beth. Pick up the phone." A pause, then a heavy, theatrical sigh. "Fine. Whatever. He was asking about you again today. Beth, he's totally hot. I mean, totally. Okay, a little rough around the edges, sure, but so what? You're not looking to marry him. I'm not even saying sleep with him, although it's not like Jake's doing all that much for you, apparently, and didn't I say I told you so about that?"

"Bitch," Beth said, fondly. Joyce had never

been one of Jake's supporters, claiming that he was too bland, too boring and too much a landlubber at heart.

"Anyway, I'm not saying touch—well, I am, but if you don't want to, then just bask a little in the attentive hotness! Because, Beth? He's *definitely* interested in you."

Another pause, another sigh. "Whatever. I'll see you next week at the town picnic. You are not allowed to miss that, even if I have to arrange for someone to lure him out of town for the day. Bye!"

A click, and Beth was left alone with her now-even-worse mood. Dylan whatshisname had apparently been sniffing after her ever since they ran in to each other—literally—at the café, and it had only gotten worse since that disaster at the diner. And everyone seemed delighted to tell her what a nice guy Dylan was. Even Jake! Although he at least wasn't saying what a great guy he was, how friendly, how talented an artist, how hard a worker, etc., ad nauseum, just that the guy had done a good job, for fair money. It was like the entire town had forgotten that they were New Englanders, that by tradition someone had to live here their entire lives to be accepted, and sometimes not even then.

No, Dylan Meridith showed up in town, without any connections or references, and he was embraced like a long-lost child.

And he decidedly, definitely was *not* a child. Not the way he looked at her. Not that he approached her directly. No, he let other people do that. He just appeared every time she went into town—no doubt alerted by his accomplices—and *watched* her.

She felt like a deer during hunting season, and she didn't like the feeling at all. It was one thing to wish for some excitement, something new and different. It was another thing entirely to have a stranger come practically stalking you: having him invading your dreams, and then lurking everywhere during your waking moments, never allowing you a moment's peace.

So what had she done about it?

Hidden, and hoped he would go away. Or find some other female to try to overwhelm, instead of her, even though the thought of him even looking at another woman, much less touching one, made her furious.

Beth stared up at the ceiling, exasperated with herself. Clearly, hiding wasn't working. And avoidance wasn't making her mood any better, either; she was more of the "confront and be damned" sort, normally.

"So confront and be damned," she said, shutting down the computer. "You're already in the mood for it."

Just making the decision made her feel better. What on earth had she been dithering about, anyway?

Because you're sort of still seeing someone, a little voice reminded her. Because you don't know this man; nobody knows this man. Because you don't like to act on impulse. Good reasons, cautious reasons.

But she had the feeling that logic and caution weren't going to help her here.

Ready to leave, she paused in front of the mirror beside the door—there more to enlarge the appearance of her office for the occasional visiting client than for personal vanity—and studied her reflection. She had put the makeup basics on that morning, out of habit: mascara and eyeliner to play up her eyes and make them seem greener, and a slick of gloss on her lips, more to keep them moist than to add any color. It was the bane of her existence as a teenager, how quickly her skin dried out even on a normal day, requiring moisturizer on a daily basis to keep her lips from cracking, but now she rarely even thought about it.

Hair, washed and—as usual—tucked behind her ears, where it feathered out slightly. She needed to either trim it, or let it grow out again. Skin, clean and healthy-looking—no cracks or blemishes to ruin her confidence, thank God for small mercies. Her eyes were reasonably bright, and not just from exhaustion, and her features hadn't developed any disfiguring lumps or bumps overnight.

She made a horrible face at herself, like a moonstruck guppy, and felt a little better. She wanted to scare the guy off, not attract him! Remember that?

Grabbing her windbreaker off the peg, she shoved her keys and wallet into the pockets, clipped her cell phone to her waist and, at the last minute, tucked a battered old Red Sox championship baseball cap on her head, to keep the sun out of her eyes. Properly arrayed, she went out in search of her target.

It wasn't really a search. The moment she left the safety of her office, she knew where to go, like a cat following the freshly enticing smell of tuna.

Sure enough, she found him on the beach—the same beach where he had been washed ashore, two weeks ago.

Anger shifted inside her as she spotted him, having to share space with a wicked sort of pleasure. She was just—only just—willing to admit that there was a warm satisfaction in being chased after. Even if she wasn't interested. Which she wasn't. Truly.

Waiting for anger to get the upper hand again, she stood back and watched him for a while. He was sitting on what looked like an overturned bucket, working at a makeshift easel made of driftwood. In jeans and a black T-shirt, he looked pretty much the same as any guy around town. Any well-formed, lean and yet nicely muscled guy around town, anyway, and there wasn't, sadly, an overabundance of them.

From the curve of his shoulders, the sprawl of his knees, she knew that he was at ease, his arms moving freely as he sketched, occasionally looked up and out over the ocean. But she knew, somehow, that he knew that she was watching. And she wondered, suddenly, if she was really the hunter…or the prey, drawn in by well-placed bait.

Damn it. There. The anger—and the caution—was back.

"You've been asking about me," she said, coming close enough to be heard without raising her voice beyond her normal tone.

He didn't jump, or show any sign of being startled, but kept making long, swooping movements with the crayon in his hand.

"I have," he replied, not looking at her.

"Why?" She had meant to sound angry, or annoyed, but to her horror, her voice came out more plaintive, more inquiring.

"Nathan said that you'd be easier to catch if you thought you were catching me. And that getting you intrigued would mean getting you annoyed, first."

Beth stopped dead, not expecting that answer at all. Well, he won points for honesty, if not style or smoothness. And Nathan was a dead man.

"Oookay. Bluntness is absolutely your strong point. But why do you want to— Wow." She had stepped close enough to see what he was drawing, and it blew everything else out of her mind, up to and including her irritation. "You're good. I mean, you're really good."

He still didn't stop drawing, and he didn't try to shield the work from her this time, either. "Yeah. I am."

He obviously had no modesty, either. But she was honest enough herself to admit that he'd earned the ego. The seascape in front of her wasn't a reproduction of the calm face the ocean was currently showing them, but the brewing of a storm just below the surface, all tightness and swells building. There was tension in the scrapings of color, suggestions of terror and damage to come, that were echoed in the flat green sky overhead. And yet, for all the menace, there was love and beauty there, too, in the depth and stillness of the waters, and the low soaring figure of a single white bird.

It moved something in her, connecting with her restlessness with an almost audible click.

He paused, a stick of dark blue in his hand, as though contemplating adding more color to the water.

"No more," she said almost involuntarily, although she knew better—knew how much she hated having someone hang over her shoulder when she was working.

"I think you're right," he said. But she got the feeling that he wasn't talking about the sketch.

"Why did you hide your work from me, before?"

He shrugged, and she got the feeling he was embarrassed. "It mattered."

"What?"

"Anyone else…they could see them. It didn't matter. I didn't care. You…it mattered what you thought. And I got scared."

That was, in its own weird way, the sweetest, sexiest thing anyone had ever said to her, and another of her defenses went down without a struggle.

"Why did you come down?" he asked her calmly, but she heard something in his voice, a faint quaver, that made her think that he wasn't as calm or indifferent as he seemed. "Not to critique my form?"

Oh, no. He did not get to play hard to get, not after dragging her here, even if he hadn't actually done any physical dragging. "It's a public beach. More, it's a public beach down the road from my home, a fact I get the feeling you know quite well."

She had been stalked. The thought should have disturbed her more than it did. But standing next to him, the anger was damned difficult to hold on to, scuttling sideways like a greased crab. In its place, she felt that restlessness, the tingle…and that, more than his attentions, made her angry all over again. She had no control over what he might or might not do, but she could damn well control her own body!

And she had no interest in being interested in some boat-losing, seemingly penniless, rough-handed handyman who was going to waltz in and then waltz out of her life. No matter how hot he was, or how beautifully he captured the sea's moods on paper. She didn't need her body deciding who she was going to get hot for, like a pet bitch in heat.

"You don't feel it?" He sounded upset, like she had insulted him, or something.

"Feel what?" Beth took an emotional step back, if not a physical one. She felt things, hoo-yah she felt things, but be damned if she was going to admit them to him.

Although to be fair, her restlessness arrived before he did, so she couldn't blame him for that, entirely.

"I thought this would be easier," he said, almost to himself, and for the first time his confident posture slumped a little.

"You know that you're not making any sense at all, right?" she said, exasperation trumping both anger and desire, and leading to an almost over-whelming urge to put her arms around him, to feel that lean body melt into her own for comfort. Why did this man make her totally unsure and yet so certain? Beth didn't like it at all, but she couldn't make her body turn and walk away.

"Hey."

A stranger's voice made them both turn. Beth didn't know why she was so surprised—it was, as she had just pointed out, a public beach, and one that was popular for joggers year-round.

But the woman who was approaching them wasn't a jogger: she was wearing a leather jacket and dark slacks, and had sunglasses on her nose, even though it wasn't all that sunny out at the moment. She was an older woman, although not in any way decrepit or even frail-looking. In fact, there was a vibe to her, an intensity, which made her seem out of place on the beach.

"You... You're Dylan Meridith?"

Beth felt Dylan tense up, without even looking at him, like the woman had said something offen-sive, even though her tone was casual, friendly. When he didn't respond, she glanced sideways, and saw that he had put down the crayon and covered the drawing pad carefully, as though he was getting ready to pack up and go home.

"That probably depends on who's asking," he said calmly. "You need a shutter rehung? A wall painted? I'm not much good with roofing or chimneys, though."

run.

Beth felt her muscles tense. She didn't like the look of this woman, and she didn't like the way she was looking at Dylan. Not like a woman looked at a man, but…well, a little like a woman looked at a man, but also like a butcher looked at a cow. That wasn't a combination that could be good, anyway.

Then the woman turned and looked at her over her sunglasses, and Beth's muscles went from tense to screaming. Those eyes were round, almost like an anime character's—and about as flat and empty of humanity as any cartoon ever was.

run. The thought had more power to it, more urgency.

"And who are you?" the woman asked, her voice an unnervingly pleased purr. "We weren't expecting you."

"I beg your pardon?" Beth's spine stiffened, and she heard her mother's coldest, most politely Yankee tones come out of her mouth. She did not like this woman, not at all. Every inch of skin on her body was warning her that the civilized veneer of suit and sunglasses hid a very real danger to her—and to Dylan. Especially to Dylan.

she's waiting on identification. they have rules; I have to confirm, somehow, I don't know how… run. before she knows for certain.

"Beth. Run." Dylan's voice was flat, uninflected,

but carried a weight of urgency behind it. The exact same way the voice in her head had sounded.

"Too late, Beth." The woman looked behind them even as Beth heard the sound of heavy feet on the sand. Two, no, three men behind them.

"Confirmation. Maybe even two for the price of one," the woman said to the newcomers. "A nice day's work."

"Run!" Dylan shouted, grabbing and pulling Beth's arm, dragging her not up the beach, but down it—toward the waves.

"Stop them! But don't damage them!" the woman yelled. Her hair whipping into her face, Beth couldn't see anything but the sand under her feet, and Dylan's hand on her arm.

"When we hit the water, swim. Don't look back, just follow me, and swim."

She was about to argue when a sharp crack sounded, and Dylan jerked to the side, dragging her with him.

"They're shooting at us!" She had never heard a gun before, not in real life, but she had no doubt whatsoever what that noise was.

"They won't hit us. They can't risk it. But they'll try to herd us, pen us somehow. They need us alive."

Beth wondered if that was supposed to be reassuring.

"Keep going," he said, a little out of breath. "And swim!"

With that advice, they hit the salty water, and he pulled her with him deeper into the waves, his fingers digging into her skin and down onto the bone until she cried out. Salt water went into her mouth as he pulled her down and she choked. His fingers let go, and she heard that voice again in her head: *swim.*

She dove into the water with an almost automatic motion, slipping below the surface of the waves and striking out into deeper water. One stroke, then two, then she lost count as she swam. Her heart pounded in her ears, the sodden weight of her clothing dragging at her and slowing her down.

this way. Something nudged her side, and she rolled away in a panic.

this way, the voice repeated in her head, and she turned blindly toward it.

trust me, and live. Something swam over her, holding her down, and she started to panic, her eyes opening underwater to see a dark shape moving in the water next to her. Not a human shape.

Not a shark. That thought came with a wave of relief, even as her mind tried to identify it. Long and rounded form, sleek and curving around her...

A dolphin? Too wide, too squared off. A seal. A seal was herding her out to sea. The impossibility of everything overwhelmed her, and a seal seemed the least of it all. Where was Dylan? What had happened to Dylan? Had they shot him, after all? The panic overtook her then, making her struggle against the current and her insistent guide.

beth. daughter of the waves. trust me, and swim. Her breathing slowed, and her arms started stroking again, her body following the dark shape through the water, rising every now and again to take a breath of air before sliding back to the safety under the surface.

It wasn't until the water cooled around her body, indicating that they had gone far offshore, that her motion slowed, and her escort allowed her to stop and tread water.

Her head broke the surface, blinking the water out of her eyes and trying to adjust to easy access to air. They weren't that far out; the figures on the beach were still visible, if small, but they clearly were not willing to follow, not without a boat.

"We're safe. For now."

You couldn't jump while treading water, but Beth made a pretty good attempt at it when Dylan's voice sounded just next to her ear. His black hair was slicked back with water the same way hers must have been, but on him it looked good. His eyes were odd-looking, like he was wearing thick lenses in them, and his skin had a flush to it that seemed at odds with how cold the water was.

"How… Who were they? They shot at us!" Now that she had a moment to breathe, panic and outrage rose in her throat. "They came for you! That woman, she knew your name, she was there and the way she looked… Who were they? And why the hell are we out here, what happened to the seal? What did you mean, she needed confirmation? Of what? And how the hell are we going to get home, with them waiting out there?"

She paused, catching her breath, and glared at him. "And if you say 'swim' I'm going to hit you."

She looked adorable, sleek and water-slicked and flushed with the effort both of swimming and anger. Dylan felt himself getting almost painfully hard again, the restlessness and adrenaline moving in another direction, one focused entirely on the female form in front of him.

He was no virgin—unlike their sea-dwelling cousins, seal-kin enjoyed sex for its own sake, not merely producing pups—but he had never been knocked over so much merely by the sight, the touch of a woman. Dry, she had been tempting enough. Sleeked with seawater, her skin moist and flushed with exertion… Imagining what she might taste like, the skin on her back, the inside of her thighs, the soft folds of her flesh…he was pretty sure the water around him started to steam a little.

Not now, damn it! With effort, he brought his mind into control of the situation, and the heat died down. A little.

"I'm sorry." He could tread water for hours, but she couldn't. He had to get her to safety. "They came for me, yes. Hunting me. It's a thing, a rule…to avoid mistakes, they have to get confirmation, somehow, before they try to take me. Us. Everything else…this really isn't the place for this discussion." He cast a look over her shoulder. The figures on the beach were fewer: they had gone to get a boat. The woman would not have come Hunting unprepared: they were running out of time.

"Please don't hit me," he said. "But we need to swim a little more."

"And then you'll explain?" She sounded, for the first time since he had met her, uncertain, lost.

The desire, the need to protect her, that had risen hot and fast on the beach, still controlled him, even more than the desire to mate. His nature would not allow her to remain in danger—but he knew enough by now to know that her nature required answers, or she would never go with him.

The moves he had thought of to woo her, human or seal-kin, were matters of instinct and heat. Explaining to this woman what he was…and now, with a Hunter on his tail, explaining that, too? He hadn't thought that far.

All right, he hadn't thought at all. It wouldn't be the first time. But he was thinking now. He had to: both their lives depended on it.

"I'll explain…everything. But first we need to get you out of the water and somewhere safer."

She couldn't argue with that, not with the sound of bullets still ringing in both their ears. Could she?

"Swim," he said again, and saw her hazel eyes darken in annoyance. She was going to argue. Impossible female. No wonder he'd been dragged so far to find her—no female he'd ever met could make him so crazy.

He couldn't help himself, he reached forward and touched his lips to her own, intending only to reassure himself that she was real, that he hadn't dreamed her up out of his fevered imagination. But the moment he touched her, everything other than that touch was forgotten: danger, explanations, confusion all fell away and there was only them, only that amazing, intoxicating touch. Her lips were cool, wet, and tasted like the sea and sand, and a hint of the lilacs that grew all around her house. She drew back, but not far, and when his hand reached up and tangled in the slick strands of her hair, drawing her closer, she didn't resist.

She didn't wrap herself around him and beg him to do sweet, rude things to her the way she had in his dreams, true, but her lips softened, sweetening until he almost forgot about the humans waiting on the shoreline for them.

Almost. But not quite.

He had to protect her. Even from himself, if need be.

He pulled away and smiled down into her now lust-bright eyes, the black lashes wet and spiky. "Swim," he told her, and pointed. "That way. Trust me."

She groaned, but followed as he let her go and started stroking out at a diagonal, away from the shore.

Hoo boy. Just…hoo. Boy. For the promise in those brown eyes, Beth would have swum the length of the pool at the Y a dozen times. Ocean swimming couldn't be that much harder, could it?

It could, and it was.

Beth was pretty sure that her arms weren't going to fall off, and her legs hadn't really turned into lead. It only felt that way. On the plus side, her worry about sharks had turned into a vague wish that one would come by and put her out of her misery. And she wished that the shark would take the man swimming alongside her first.

Then her body warned her that the water was warming, the bottom coming closer. They were coming up on a bank of some sort.

By the time her exhausted brain processed that, her legs had kicked sand rather than water, and her hand came down on something hard. Land. Rock, crumbling under her fingers. "Thank you, thank you, thank you," she chanted under her breath, crawling on hands and knees onto the solid surface, not caring how the rough edges tore at her sodden jeans or the skin of her palms.

Once she was entirely out of the water, she collapsed onto her stomach, too tired to even roll over. She spent a few thoughts toward trying to figure out where they were, what outcropping of rocks they had come up on, but the effort was too much to continue. Much better to lie there and just breathe. At this point, someone could have come along with a gun, and she might have welcomed being put out of her misery.

There was the wet slapping noise of someone flopping down beside her. Dylan. She knew, even without opening her eyes. That warm body, already instantly recognizable to her, even cooled by the water, could be no one else.

"Talk," she said, not looking at him. If she looked at him, talking might not be all they did.

"Now?" He sounded surprised, and not even a little winded, the bastard.

"Now." It wasn't like she had the strength to do anything else other than listen, anyway. No matter what delicious sinfulness his eyes might be promising. "Who were they? Why were they after you? After me? What's going on?"

"You're not going to believe me."

She almost laughed. "Do they teach you guys that line in guy school, or something? When we're off learning about tampons and breasts, you guys learn lines?"

From the corner of her eye she saw a supine shrug, and a piece of wet black hair flopped into his eyes. "I don't know. I've never been to school."

That didn't surprise her, entirely. He didn't give off college-guy vibes at all; too...not hard, *hard* was the wrong word—or maybe not, she thought, remembering the feel of him in the water—but rough, ragged. Smart, but like it all came firsthand, burns, bumps and bruises. Now that she let herself get past the immediate reactions his presence brought out in her, she could feel it in him, like the texture of leather when you expected plush.

She never thought that she'd find a guy like that appealing; she had always, carelessly, demanded a certain level of sophistication and education from the men she dated, even casually.

But Dylan didn't seem uneducated, either. And he had to have taken art classes, to draw the way he did, even with natural talent. But then why...

"You're trying to distract me," she realized, finally finding the strength to turn her head to glare at him.

He made a soft, silky noise that came from deep in his chest. "I am. It almost worked."

"Almost doesn't count," she retorted automatically, ignoring the desire to reach out and touch his skin, or run her fingers through his still-wet hair. The words had the feel of an old argument, one she had never had before. Now that she wasn't running from him, he wasn't not-chasing her, it all felt so familiar, so well-established, so...weird.

He didn't seem to notice anything, weird or otherwise. "They were Hunters. I think. I've never run in to them before but I've heard of them. We're warned about them, when we go inland. It's always a risk, I just...I don't know how they found me."

He sounded frustrated and annoyed more than scared, as though having someone shooting at him was an annoyance, not a threat. And yet, he had dragged her off into the water in a damn-sure hurry, and she didn't think it was just to avoid talking.

"Hunters. On Nantucket?" She wasn't quite buying that. "Not many deer out here. Unless they were hunting rabbits?"

"Only two-legged ones."

She felt her own mouth twist in an unwanted smile. They had rabbited pretty fast, true.

He sat up and pulled his T-shirt off, grimacing at the clammy fabric, and tossed it onto a rock to dry in the sunlight. "I hate clothing."

The sight of his bare chest, and the thought of him shedding all his clothing and reclining in nothing but that creamy-smooth bare skin, sent her mind somewhere that had nothing to do with their current situation, and she forced herself to stop wondering if his legs had that same muscled sleekness, and what they would feel like pressed against her own.

"Distractions. Not working," she told him.

They were, all too well. But she was going to stay focused.

Dylan was still talking out loud, and she got the feeling that he was running it through in his own mind more than he was explaining anything to her. "You had never seen her before. She didn't know who you were, didn't greet you. I've only been around here for a few weeks, but even I know that meant that she was a stranger—not even a regular tourist. And she was looking for me. By name. Something about how I reacted to her was what she was looking for, but she didn't approach me until then, until she was ready to make her move."

"And that—the fact that she was pretty much stalking you—made you nervous. Hell, it made you run. Way before she brought out the goons with guns. Who are you?" Beth swallowed, suddenly aware that she was on a totally isolated islet with a man she knew nothing about—not even if the name he was using was actually his own. "Who the hell was she?" *What have you gotten yourself into, Elizabeth?*

"Don't be afraid." He didn't look at her; in fact, he was carefully looking away as he said it. "You should never be afraid of me. I could never hurt you. I would die for you."

The words were so simply, so sincerely said, Beth found herself believing him. She believed that he would die rather than hurt her, die rather than allow her to be hurt. Insane. He was probably insane, and she had to be, to trust him, but what other choice did she have?

I would die for you, beloved.

She refused to listen to her imagination, instead focusing on what he was actually saying.

"That woman, the men with her, they're Hunters. And they hunt my people." He paused, as though he was going to say something more, and then shook his head. His hair was still wet, unlike hers, which was drying quickly in the light breeze. An advantage to short hair.

Yeah. Insane. But play the cards you're dealt, Beth. "Your people. Why?"

"We have something they want. Something they hunt."

God, it was like pulling teeth with a string! She snapped. "Dylan, I just got shot at! I just had to swim—what, two, three miles?—out into the ocean with a total stranger. My cell phone is ruined, my wallet is a soggy mess, God knows if my shoes will recover, and okay, that's shallow but it bothers me! So, damn it, I want answers!"

He let out a strange bark that might have been laughter, or annoyance. "They want our skins."

Whatever she had been expecting, it wasn't that.

Chapter 7

Dylan's words echoed over the sound of the wavelets riding the shore, and the wind, and the distant screaming of the gulls overhead.

Skins.

She was being hunted for her skin. By people. Those people. That woman. For her skin.

The weight of that statement sank into her brain, and despite the fact that she knew all the words, and they were in a perfectly reasonable order, spoken in clear English, she didn't quite comprehend what he had said at first. She just sat there and blinked at him, waiting for the punch line to arrive, for someone to step out from behind the curtain and explain what the hell was going on.

It didn't come, not the punch line or the explanation. Dylan just sat there as well, perched on the rocks in his damp jeans and irritatingly, enticingly bare chest and beautifully arched bare feet, and watched her watching him. In the two weeks since he had arrived, his pale skin had turned a faint caramel from the sun, toffee and cream with only the faintest dappling of hair across his chest and down his arms. Not quite a six-pack under that smooth skin, but firm and flat, and as she watched a muscle twitched across his abdomen, as though flinching from the touch of her gaze.

Skin. Her skin. Not her, not Beth-who-was-a-person. Just the shell, the sausage casing. Beth looked at her arm, at the still water-wrinkled fingers, the chapped and sun-pinked skin of her forearm. Skin?

Four hours ago she had woken in her own bed, in her own home, and the world wasn't perfect but it made sense. A lot could happen in four hours.

Everything could change, in four hours.

Her shoulders shook, and she wasn't sure if she was holding back hysteria, or hysterical laughter, but it was definitely bubbling up inside. On the plus side, she wasn't twitchy or out of sorts anymore. That had to be something, right?

"I'm sorry." Dylan made a movement as though to touch her, then changed his mind and reached over and tested his shirt instead. It obviously hadn't dried enough to satisfy him, because he adjusted it in a different way on the rock and then turned back to her. The wet denim clung to his ass in ways that really should have been illegal. Even reeling from what he had just told her, impossible as it was, and jolted by the excess adrenaline from their swim, to say nothing of the shock of being shot at, Beth couldn't help wishing he had taken off his jeans, as well. Were his legs more heavily furred, or smooth? And did that make a difference to the value of *his* skin?

The thought was totally insane. Her mind and her body had clearly parted company a long time ago.

No, not so long ago. Just two weeks ago when this crazy man washed up on the beach of her town and started chasing after her. Except he hadn't actually done any chasing. What was it he had said, that Nathan—that turncoat—had said she would be easier to entice than chase? Hah! Nathan was going to get kicked in the shin, next time she went into Apollo's.

Right now she was pissed off at everyone who had anything to do with Dylan Meridith and his seemingly out-of-the-blue obsession with her.

Oddly enough, all the apprehension she had felt earlier, the feeling of being trapped and hunted, had disappeared the moment someone actually *was* hunting her. Sitting next to him, bedraggled, confused and wondering if she had lost her mind, her reaction to that crazy man was totally undiluted by distrust, either of him or herself. All she wanted to do was find a patch of softer sand somewhere, and…

And do things that were totally, insanely inappropriate, all things considered. What was *with* her hormones? Apparently, being threatened and dumped into the ocean with a crazy man was what got her juices going. If she'd only known that in college…

Definitely hysterical laughter, yes. A burp of sound escaped her, and she stuffed the back of her hand into her mouth to keep anything worse from coming out.

Focus, Miss Elizabeth. She could almost hear Ben's voice, implacable as the rocks they were sitting on. *Live, first. Figure out what's going on, and how to get out of it, skin still attached. Then worry about your crazy hormones.*

"Right." She shoved the laughter down and used both hands to swipe at her hair, trying to finger-comb the tangled strands before they dried too badly. "Sorry for what?" she was finally calm enough to ask Dylan, focusing on his face so that she wasn't staring at his body. Not much help there—she was still in overload. "You didn't shoot at me. You dragged me out here, yeah, but there was no shooting involved." No, why the hell was she excusing him? He was the one who got her into this!

Beth placed the heels of her palms against her eyes and pressed, as though that would make everything fall back into shape when she looked at the world again.

"I got you into this," he said, echoing her thoughts. "If I hadn't come here, they would never have found you."

She risked looking. He was slumped on the edge of a rounded rock and, as she watched, ran his hands through his own hair, a gesture of frustration and annoyance. "That's my fault. I didn't think. It was all rush and rush, and wanting and not thinking. I always do that. And that's probably why they found me, because I forgot everything I knew except finding you."

He turned his face up to her then, and the sweet brown of his eyes made her want to forgive him everything he had ever done.

She wasn't that far gone, though. He might be sorry, but he wasn't wrong. It was all his fault. Focus on that, Beth, she reminded herself. Don't lose sight of the facts.

"I need to get you somewhere safe," he went on. "We need to go somewhere safe. But I don't know where. I can't take you home—that will lead them right to the colony. I can't do that." He stood and started pacing, muttering to himself. "Damn it. Damn, damn. Think, second-born, think!"

Hunters. After her skin. His skin first, from what he said, and hers as an added plus. Those were facts, too, if she bought into his story. She looked at her arm again, wondering what it might be worth, and to whom. And why. It made no sense. None of this had ever made any sense.

But there was something beyond the confusion, something deeper than the sexual zing she felt every time she looked at Dylan. She had been scuttling around it, avoiding it the way she had avoided him. Avoiding the dreams that had only begun the night he was washed up on the island, the restlessness than began with the storm that brought him into her life, too.

Something was happening. She couldn't avoid it, deny it, any longer.

A connection. Something between the two of them… Something that made her believe…not in his story, exactly, but that he would not hurt her. That whatever he was doing, it was to protect her. That he *knew* her, and she knew him. Not just now, but always. Before they were born, and long after they died, cycles upon cycles.

It was a strange feeling. She had been independent since she was sixteen, and Ben and Glory agreed that she was capable of running her own life. She had taken care of herself, done everything she needed on her own. Even Jake had never taken care of her—he assumed that if she wanted something, she got it or did it herself, or did without.

The knowledge—and she *knew,* now—that Dylan would do anything for her, would go miles out of his way to satisfy her, was…humbling. Sweet, and terrifying.

"You're in danger," she said, as though it were a sudden revelation.

"What? Yeah. We have to go somewhere safe. Somewhere they won't think to look for us. But I don't know…" He looked up again, his eyes now anguished. "I don't know your world. I don't know where to go, that they won't anticipate."

"Inland."

She spoke without thinking, then closed her eyes and shook her head, thinking it through. That was her strength: if he rushed and reacted, she sat back and thought. "You went to the sea, instinctively. They didn't expect that, or they were unprepared, otherwise they would have come at us with a boat, too."

"They didn't think I'd risk it, changing voluntarily, where they could reach me," he said softly, but it didn't make any sense to her. She waited, but he didn't say anything more.

"That woman, you said she was playing by rules, that she needed to follow procedures?"

Dylan nodded, his entire body leaning forward now, as he listened intently to her thought process.

"If that's the way she thinks, she's used to going by what's done, not improvising. So now I bet she's thinking about nothing except the water routes, thinking that since it worked once, you'll stick to that. They will expect you to feel comfortable out here. So you won't stay out here."

"*We* won't," he corrected her.

"What?" Her eyes opened suddenly, and she slewed around to stare at him.

"You missed the part when they included you in their agenda?" He tried for joking, but didn't pull it off. "We're in this together. You and me."

The words were tough, but the look in his eye suddenly was anything but. The anguish was still there, and the worry, but something sharper, with more spice, turned the brown into hot gold that made her think of other things—more pleasurable things—they could do together. *You and me.* Whatever she was feeling, she wasn't alone with it.

Getting dunked and shot at turned him on, too. She supposed that was good to know.

Suddenly it was very important that she know one thing for certain. "Dylan. When you say skin, do you mean that metaphorically, or…"

"Actual skins. Without us in them," he clarified for her, his brown eyes watching her steadily for…what? She hadn't given him enough of a reaction already?

"Oh." Yeah. That was what she had thought, but she had wanted to be sure. The "why" suddenly seemed less important—she had a strong suspicion she wouldn't care about what they were going to do with her skin, once she was out of it.

Beth sat for a moment longer, then stood, wincing as her socks still squelched wetly inside her shoes. That whole skinless image put a kibosh on her libido for the moment, anyway. Nice to know.

"Are you…all right?" the object of her libido's exertions asked, looking at her from his rock-perch, those brown eyes still liquid and irresistible.

"All right? You think I should be all right?" She was so far from all right she wasn't even on the same planet anymore. She was so far from all right she had come around again, and everything was just wicked fine and dandy.

"You're not all right." He sounded miserable. "I never wanted… I'm sorry."

"Dylan." God, the man just melted her, even when she was furious. "No more sorry, okay? Let's just…deal with this. Okay?"

He swallowed hard, his throat contracting tightly. "All right."

She gave him what she hoped was an encouraging smile. "I don't suppose you could whistle up a boat, so we don't have to swim all the way back to the island?"

Or, worse yet, all the way to the mainland, because there was no way she could manage that.

"Whistle? No." He had an odd look in his eyes now, like he was thinking of something far away, something he couldn't believe he hadn't remembered before. Then he smiled, and the wicked joy in that toothy grin was a revelation. "But I might be able to sing up something."

Beth quickly discovered that he wasn't joking. The islet they were on was barely enough rock to earn the name, and he went out on to the farthest spar of rock, perching on it like an oversize gull, telling her to wait on the more comfortable shore.

The wind was in a lull, but it still carried back to her bits and pieces of the music he was, literally, singing. It was wordless, atonal, and should have been unpleasant, but reminded her instead of the whines and hums whales used to communicate. She wondered briefly if he was going to call up a whale to swallow them whole, like Jonah, and recognized the signs of hysteria bubbling back up. Skins. What would her skin be worth? Why would anyone want it? Was she going to be stuffed like an elk over a fireplace? Or used as somebody's sick idea of luxury car upholstery?

Or…each idea was worse than the last, and she
was getting close to curling up in a ball and going
totally nonresponsive. Rather than give in to it, or
the fear of those…Hunters that was nibbling at the
corners of her mind, she got up and made herself
useful. It had rained a few days before—maybe
one of these rocks had preserved a puddle of water
they could drink.

There wasn't much to see—the entire islet was
barely the size of her house, most of it underwater,
and nothing more than some mosslike plants grew
on the rocks. One bad storm and the entire thing
would be awash. Luckily for them, the weather was
calm and clear.

On the other side of the islet she got lucky, discovering a shallow rock under the overhang of another
that had collected enough rainwater to be useful.
Using hands to cup it would waste too much, between
the splashing and the inevitable spilling, so she got
down on her hands and knees and lapped at it, just
enough to remoisten her mouth and feel her brain
cool down a little. Water helped. Food would help
more; she hadn't stopped for breakfast before coming
down to the beach, and the swim had tightened her
stomach sharply. Whatever craziness that man did to
her insides, it wasn't affecting her appetite, at least.

When Dylan was done doing whatever it was he
was doing, she would tell him about the water hole.
And then they would figure out which direction
they would need to swim in.

A bird circled overhead, and she shaded her eyes

and looked up at it. "Lucky bird, having wings," she said. "And you, woman, if you still smoked, you could have lit a fire and called for help that way." Of course, the swim would have ruined any matches or lighter she had on her, and if she still smoked she would not have been able to swim out this far in the first place, probably. So useless all around.

The bird dipped its wings and flew away, and she went back to find out what Dylan was up to.

"Gave up, huh?" she asked, on seeing him back on the rocky beach they had been sitting on. Then her jaw fell open in shock at what rested just above the wavelets lapping against the shore: a small canoe, painted garish pink like something from a Barbie Goes Camping kit. A frayed rope dangled from the bow, evidence that it had come loose from a tie-up on some dock somewhere.

"No paddles," Dylan said apologetically, like he was embarrassed that he hadn't been able to present her with a yacht, skipper and chef to go with it. "But I figured we could improvise."

This time, when the laughter came, she let it.

"Elizabeth?"

She waved off his concern, letting the tears run down her face unchecked. He looked unconvinced, but sat next to her and held her hand in his own, patting it occasionally, until she was done.

"All right." She wiped her eyes one last time and sighed. "No paddles, huh?"

* * *

"Damn, damn and thrice damn." The Hunter paced up and down the sidewalk in front of her car, a completely innocuous dark blue sedan with the engine of a race car. Like the Hunters themselves, it was designed to blend into any surroundings, to not excite any notice, to disappear when someone looked for it. It was designed to be successful, not idling, wasting time and money while the prey escaped and clients agitated for results. The sort of people they had for clients, you did not want them agitated.

Her cell phone was in her hand, but rather than placing a call, she was slapping it against her thigh in rhythm to her pacing. What a mess, a total and unmitigated mess. Two of her team had gone back to the village to check the bed-and-breakfast the selkie had been staying in, but it was a wasted effort, she knew that already; the creature wouldn't go there once it had gotten away. Once in the ocean, it would have retaken its natural form, slipping on the waves to safety, out of their reach.

She blamed herself for that; foolish to have confronted it on the beach, a novice Hunter's mistake, but the timing had seemed right. After ten days of studying its movements, she had determined that it was predictable in its behavior, like most of its kind. During the day it was in the village, interacting, and in plain sight. She needed it alone, caught off guard and without the protective coloring of humans around it. The early-morning walks on the beach had looked perfect: there would be no distractions, no witnesses and no one to interfere with her contact-and-confirmation. The woman's presence looked to be a problem at first, and then a surprising godsend—the creature seemed protective of her, which would limit its options. That had been her idea, anyway.

"Damn it," she swore again, putting the phone away and narrowly resisting the urge to kick the nearest tire. She should have had the men shoot the damn thing, and be damned the possible damage to the hide. Or, better yet, to shoot the woman, keep it from reaching the water. That was the second rule hammered into them during training: never, ever let the prey reach water. Once in its seal-form, a selkie was useless to them—it was the transition that was important, the transition where the human skin could be taken and made useful. Once the beast was in seal form, a Hunter had no leverage, no access to the magic that made the beasts so valuable.

But she had held off, afraid to damage the skins beyond use. That was the unforgivable sin, even more than allowing escape—making the skins unharvestable, unusable. Once a target was confirmed, even a bruise on the skin was considered the mark of an amateur. A tear or rip in the hide, and the shape-change would not work on the client, making it nothing more than mediocre upholstery.

And so she had held off, properly, and in any other situation, the Hunt would have been over, her shot at the major leagues gone. Alone, the selkie would have slid into the waves, disappeared and been lost to them. But it had taken the woman along. A woman with the same feel as all the others of the breed, enough that she'd thought at first there were two for the bagging, doubling her profit from this Hunt. Unfortunately, they had seen her swimming in the waves in human form, so she wasn't a shape-changer, despite the similarity in appearances. Interesting. A half-breed, maybe? There had always been rumors that they could breed with humans, but as far as she knew it had never been proven one way or the other.

The woman shrugged, letting the question go. She snapped her fingers, and one of her remaining men stepped forward, ready for orders. "Call in a helicopter. Now!" A boat would be useless: there was too much area to cover. It would be expensive, in money and favors, to call in a copter, but from the air they would be able to scout the surface, hopefully spot them before they reached any sort of safe haven. With the woman swimming, even if the male had changed form, they couldn't have gone far.

Two of the men who came with her stayed on the beach, their eyes scanning the immediate area, their hands never straying far from their now-holstered weapons. She snorted. Gun-happy idiots. Even the best shot couldn't guarantee only a flesh wound. That was the first thing they learned: dead, a selkie was nothing more than a curiosity. They needed to be alive in order to give up their skins. If she had a decent team, a *trained* team…

If, if and if. Useless damn conjecture. There weren't as many Hunters as there once were. That was a simple, inescapable fact. Fewer retired soldiers, fewer ex-mercenaries, fewer people with the guts to do what needed to be done, to get the job done. So she had book-trained desk jockeys fumbling in the field, and only a handful of them she would want to have to depend on in a crunch.

Never mind. They would do the job she set them to, and she would do the rest. That was why she was Hunt Leader.

As Hunt Leader, she also had to do the unpleasant things as well as the enjoyable. With one last scowl at the water line, she flipped open her phone and pressed the first number on her speed dial.

"Sir." She took off her sunglasses while speaking, as though her boss could see her. "Yes, sir. There has been a slight change in the plans. I may need to expand the scope of the Hunt."

Chapter 8

Afterward, all that Beth could remember of the long, painful paddle back to shore was how her shoulders ached, and that the makeshift driftwood paddle cut into her hands, leaving a long red scratch across her palm. Her brain seemed to have shut down in the aftermath of Dylan's revelations.

Skins. Hunters. Her.

Why her? Why him? Why would anyone want their skin?

The only things she could come up with were so sick, so insane, she...she could believe them, because people were sick and cruel and did things that humans shouldn't do. But this...didn't feel like that. Like some kind of dark, twisted "National Weird News" headline. It felt...

Surreal. Strange. But Dylan was taking it so calmly, more annoyed that he had been caught off guard than horrified by the very idea, that Beth found herself following his lead, staying calm and focusing on getting back to the mainland.

She still wasn't sure what to think—how often do you get told there is someone, or a bunch of someones, out there who thinks of you like a particularly exotic coat?—but when it came down to deciding between a possibly crazy man who saved your life and a crazy woman who ordered people to shoot at you, and was maybe going to skin you? She'd take the one not shooting, every day.

The fact of the matter was, whatever craziness Dylan had, he was protecting her from worse.

"Land." His voice was low, barely carrying the short distance from the stern of the canoe to the bow. "Over there."

She had been so deep in thought, in concentrating on not noticing the soreness in her arms and back, that she hadn't even realized they were coming into a small, undeveloped harbor.

"Do you know where we are?"

She shook her head. "No. I'm not used to seeing the coastline from this side. My family…we weren't much for sailing."

"Huh." There was the sound of the makeshift driftwood oar hitting the side of the canoe, and he shifted, making the small craft shudder under the change in balance. "Ship your oar, let me take us in."

She put her own bit of driftwood across her lap

thankfully, not even minding when cold salty water dripped onto her legs. At this point, a little more water wasn't going to make any difference. And it was surprisingly nice, sitting back and letting Dylan pilot them in, his smooth stroke propelling the canoe over the waves into the shallow water, coming up on the sandy beach with a final surge.

She started to climb out, and her legs buckled under her. Dylan was there, his arms under her knees, swinging her up into a scoop carry, so that her arms automatically went around his neck, her cheek resting against his chest.

"You did great," his voice assured her, but it was the feel of his body against hers, supporting her, that made her actually believe it. Skin to skin, she didn't think he could lie to her.

He deposited her gently onto the sand, then waded back out with one hand on the rim of the canoe, pushing it against the waves until the little pink boat was caught up in the retreating water, floating out toward the open ocean.

"For the next person who might have need," he said, almost apologetically, when he came and collapsed next to her.

"Yeah." She had no idea what he was talking about and didn't much care. He had gotten them onto dry land with a pink canoe and no navigational tools other than some sort of inner compass. In her book, he was a big damn hero.

"So what now?"

He shook his head. "I have no idea."

All right, he was a big damn hero with limits. That was all right. He might know about…whatever he knew about, but she was the land-dweller here.

The term came naturally into her mind, and she hesitated. There was something she knew, or should know…a story her father had told her and Tal, when they were very young, maybe, or a book she had read…

It didn't matter, wasn't important. Stories would wait until they were somewhere safe.

"We can't go to the authorities," Dylan said. "Not until we know how they found me. They could have connections anywhere, but probably they heard about my being washed up through the police, or…" He paused, and a look of pain washed across his face. "Or the clinic."

"No police about the people who're shooting at us. Right. Great. We need to go under their radar, at least until we have an idea who we can trust, and time to come up with a real plan. My credit cards are probably ruined—" that long in salt water was ruinous "—but we shouldn't use them, anyway. Or my ATM card, either. I've watched enough TV to know that's the easiest way to track someone and it sounds like these people've got too much insider information already. So, short of mugging somebody, we're stuck with whatever cash we've got on hand."

Dylan dug into his front pocket, pulling out a wad of bills that were much the worse for being drenched in salt water and then drying in his pocket. "I have…four hundred dollars?"

Beth swallowed hard—who carried that much money on them, so casually?—and then hid her shock and relief in an equally casual acceptance of the information. "That will do for a bit. We need to find a place to get new clothing, some food, because I for one am about to collapse with hunger—" and her stomach growled right on cue "—and we need a place to stay long enough to figure out what we're going to do next."

She thought about adding "and we need to call the cops" to her list, but stopped. Not because she didn't intend to do that, no matter what her big damn hero said, but because she needed to do it in a way that left Dylan out of the story. Whatever was going on, however he had landed on the town beach two weeks ago, clearly he was off the grid, and wanted to keep it that way. Whatever sick game he was part of, with Hunters and skin-stealing, and carrying large amounts of cash earned under the table doing handyman work... She owed him that much, at least, to keep the cops off his back if that was what he wanted. Even if he was a crazy man, and this was all his fault.

"Come on." She stood up and tested her legs. They were shaky, but managed to support her, so she reached out to encourage Dylan up. He, annoyingly, stood without any obvious difficulty.

"We're footing it?"

She had never heard the term before, but knew exactly what he meant. "Yep."

The beach was a narrow one, barely worthy of the name, like any of a hundred little inlets. A sign at the end told them that they were on State property, and that fishing with a permit was allowed between the hours of 4:00 a.m. and 7:00 a.m. There was a graveled turnoff, and a narrow dirt road without any signs or indications as to where it led. Beth paused, realizing that she didn't even know where they had landed. It wasn't Nantucket or Martha's Vineyard, but it might have been Cape Cod—or maybe they had gone all the way around to the mainland?

"Only game in town," Dylan said, letting go of her hand and shoving his into the pocket of his jeans, staring down the road like it was paved with burning hot stones.

"Yeah." She couldn't work up any enthusiasm, either. But curling up on the sand wasn't an option.

They walked a mile or two along the road until it joined up with a paved one, and hailed a passing pickup truck. The driver, a grizzled man in his fifties, took one look at them and started laughing, but a story about an overturned canoe and car keys lost at the bottom of the bay earned them the right to pile into the back of the truck for a short drive to the nearest shopping plaza.

"Thank God for Target," Beth said, staring up at the familiar red sign with mixed disbelief and relief and walking through the electronic sliding doors. The sudden immersion in noise and bustle, normally annoying, was like music to her ears, and she stood there for a moment, just enjoying it. A world with Target was normal, familiar.

Dylan touched her arm, and she turned and accepted a wad of bills from him to supplement the thirty dollars she had found in her own ruined wallet. "All right, I'll meet you back here in an hour?"

He looked a little taken aback at being abandoned in the front of the store, and Beth almost laughed. She would finish her shopping and come back to find him—she suspected that he would still be standing there, looking helplessly at socks, or maybe distracted by the electronics department. Typical guy, no matter where he came from.

She kept her own shopping simple: two pairs of jeans, a package of cotton underwear and one of plain white socks, a dark blue sweatshirt without a logo and a pair of plain white sneakers. If someone was actually hunting them, the last thing she wanted to do was give anyone anything to remember.

Thinking of that, she added a denim baseball cap and a pair of sunglasses to her cart. Clichéd, but useful.

She made her purchases, then sat down on a bench and switched to new socks and sneakers. She dumped the old shoes into the bag, thinking that she might be able to salvage them, and went in search of Dylan.

He was already standing in line to check out, she was surprised and pleased to see.

"Get everything you need?"

"Yes, mother," he replied semi-seriously. She leaned over and investigated his cart. He must watch the same television shows she did, because he had gone the same route: clean plain clothing without any logos or obvious flash, although his sneakers were actual running shoes, complete with stripes, and a pair of black sweatpants.

He also had a six-pack of Coke, a large bag of beef jerky and a gallon of bottled water, plus two oversize beach towels and a knapsack.

"Looks like you covered everything," she said dryly. "I don't know what I was thinking, going off without my towel."

He gave her a blank look, and she just shook her head. "Never mind. Pay, and let's get out of here. There's a diner across the parking lot, and if I don't get food in me soon, even that jerky's going to start to look good."

"I like jerky." He sounded as defensive as a little boy scolded for hoarding frogs.

"Good. You eat it. I want a hamburger. With bacon. And fries. And coffee. And maybe even a hot-fudge sundae. I'm *starving*."

She was. Her normal appetite was healthy, but this was overwhelming.

With their purchases in his new bag, fresh clothing on their bodies and food on the table in front of them, Dylan still wasn't able to relax. Not because he thought the Hunters were still after them—he knew they were, but there was time to eat before they had to move on. No, his nerves had less to do with them, and more to do with the woman shoveling a cheeseburger with bacon into her mouth with an appetite that made him wonder if she would be that hungry in other appetites, as well. Now that the immediate danger had passed, the urgency had returned. He wasn't quite at the stage of taking her on the table…but he wanted to.

She wiped her mouth with a napkin and looked across the table. "You're staring at me."

"I like the way you eat."

He also liked the way a flush ran up her neck, all the way to her ears, when he said something that embarrassed her. It didn't show on her face, just her neck. It made him want to follow the path with his tongue, from collarbone to the delicate area just behind the rounded lobe of her ear.…

He forced those thoughts out of his head with an effort and went back to eating his own steak and eggs. Protein. Keep the brain working, not the cock. He couldn't woo his mate if they were both skinned and mounted.

All right, wrong word choice. Dylan shifted uncomfortably and tried to think of the most disgusting shark carcass he had ever seen wash up onshore.

"Are you okay?"

"Yeah," he muttered, knowing he was flushing as badly as she was. "I'm fine."

"Do you think…do you think they can find us here?"

"Yes." He risked looking up and saw her face scrunch in worry and a hint of fear. He had to make that fear go away. "But not right away. It's okay.

You were right, they'll search the coastline first. So long as we head away, right away, we should be able to stay ahead of them."

The thought of leaving the security and familiarity of the water made his voice shake, but he hoped Beth would not notice it. She was right; there was no choice. If he stayed, they would find him. If they found him...he was reasonably brave, and death wasn't a terrifying thought to him, but that was not the way he wanted to go. And if he were Hunted, who would protect Beth? She didn't even know what she was, much less why anyone would want to kill her....

And he had to tell her. Before anything else. Before he could woo her. He had to tell her who— what—she was.

That—that one thought—scared him more than an entire pack of Hunters. She didn't know, had been kept in ignorance of her heritage, which meant that her family probably didn't know, all the way back to the grandfather who came from the ocean. It was unheard-of, but there it was. Who knew what might happen once she knew? He couldn't even imagine. She might...she might turn away from him, in shock, or disgust or...

"I'm sorry I got you into this. I... It wasn't what I was intending. I didn't know."

"Didn't know what?" She put the last bit of her hamburger down and used a French fry to scoop some ketchup off her plate.

"That you were...like me. I didn't know you at

all, it was just…" He dropped his fork and sank his face into his hands, almost laughing at how impossible all of this was.

"Dylan?" Her voice, her lovely silken wind-tossed voice, the same sound he had heard on the shore that first night, bypassing his ears and going straight into his soul. His heart rose to it, even as his cock did the same.

my mate.

"What?"

She had heard him. The tone of her voice changed, making that much obvious. The same way she must have heard him urging her to swim, to keep swimming, except that now she had no way to pretend it was anything other than what it was.

Proof, if he needed it, that he had chosen correctly. Not that he doubted.

"My mate," he said, looking up and meeting her gaze squarely. "I came looking for my mate. I came…washed literally to your doorstep, and there is nothing but Fate in that."

He winced at the rhyme, but held her gaze, watching as her irises widened in shock and—he hoped—shared awareness and arousal.

"I sensed you, even in my village, miles away. I could taste you in the wind, feel you in the water. You drew me unerring as the tide and constant as the waves. And all the time I thought I was leaving the familiar, leaving the known, only to discover you…long-lost and dreaming of me, as well. Long-lost, but kin."

"Kin?" Her voice was soft, lost in the picture he was drawing with his words.

Once you're in deep water, all you can do is swim, and hope you make safely it to land. "Sea-kin, you're called. A daughter born on land, but to the sea. That's why you are in danger from the Hunters, as well as me. I don't know why your great-grandfather brought his children up onto the shore, all those years ago. For their safety? To please his land-born wife? I don't know. But the sea remained in your blood, waiting. Waiting for me."

"Waiting… Wait a minute." Her eyes narrowed, and he discovered that Beth Havelock intent was even more arousing than Beth Havelock dreamy. "Just…wait a minute. Waiting? Mate? What the hell are you talking about? And kin to what?"

The moment of truth, and Dylan forced the words out, despite his fear. "My people. Seal-kin. Landers—humans—call us selkies."

Beth believed him. She didn't know why, but she believed him. It made no sense; he was a crazy man. A hotter-than-hot crazy man, but crazy nonetheless. The people shooting at them were probably doctors, using tranquilizer guns to bring him back to the loony bin. Weren't there studies that said artistic ability and being nuts were often found together? She remembered reading that somewhere, once.

But she looked into his deep brown eyes, listened to his voice, and believed him. No: more than believed, worse than believed. She *knew*. The dreams, the stories her father used to tell...the feeling of restlessness, and the sense that she could trust him, could let herself drown in him, that she'd never felt with anyone before...

"Selkies." The word sounded strange, felt strange to say.

"Seal-kin," he corrected her, then relented. "Selkies. Yes."

"Seal-kin. As in, like...you're not human." That was freaking her out, overriding the sense of comfort briefly as half-remembered bits of *Creature from the Black Lagoon* ran wildly in the back of her memory. Not that Dylan looked anything at all like that. Not even anything like *The Island of Dr. Moreau. Cat People,* maybe. She watched too many old movies. "Are you? Or..."

"That's...never really been settled," he told her, picking up the last bit of steak on his fork and eating it, thinking as he chewed and swallowed. "Physically, we're human. We obviously can breed with humans—otherwise your entire family wouldn't exist. The legends say..." He paused, obviously trying to remember the old stories. "The legends vary, depending on the culture, and whatever fit best with the belief system of the human population telling them. They go back into prehistory, most of them. But the story I was told is simpler, and not quite so ancient." His voice took on a storytelling, singsong quality. "Once, hundreds of generations ago, a sailing ship foundered off the coast of an unnamed land. All hands were thought to be lost, and their families mourned.

"But not all died in the cold waters. Several— good sailors, who knew the sea, and knew how to placate her, with kind treatment and smooth sailing—were rescued by Neptune's children, Tethys's children, whatever your preferred mythology…the dolphins and the seals."

"Water mammals," Beth said, nodding. That made sense. You couldn't grow up near the water, in a sailing community, without hearing stories of dolphins who were reported to have saved drowning sailors, although as far as she knew they were all just urban—aquatic?—legends….

"Yes. Kin. Distant, perhaps, but…not entirely unalike. Ones who came out of the sea, and returned again."

Beth nodded, absently reaching for another fry and eating it. They, dolphins, that is, and whales, had evolved hands, and given them up for flippers again, preferring the ocean to the land; she remembered that theory from somewhere.

"Some of those sailors found new berths in other ports, taking sail once again," Dylan went on. "But others…stayed with the kin, and grew to understand them, to comprehend them and their ways. And…changed, with that understanding. And they eventually brought wives to that understanding, and raised their children with the kin-pups, and both sides of that generation grew together as one….

"And so the seal-kin were established, and grew

into myth. Or maybe the myth grew into them. Either is possible, I suppose."

There was something in that story he wasn't telling, and she wasn't going to ask. If there was actual seal-blood in the mix somewhere, it went from being semiplausible to totally impossible, and she'd have to call the men with the butterfly nets on both of them.

"And my great-whatever-grandfather?" Her grandmother had died before Beth was born, her grandfather only a faint, shuffling memory, standing on the widow's walk, looking out over the moonlit waves, while her father wrapped his arms around her, and told her stories about the stars.

"He came from the sea, with his wife and children, and never again set foot in water...but never left it entirely, either?" That was the gossip, and gossip was as good as history, in seafaring towns.

"Selkie." It was half question, half statement.

"I can see it, *feel* it in you. So...yes."

"And these Hunters...they want us, want our skin? Because...we're selkies?"

"More or less." He dodged the question. "Hunters hunt what is rare. We're quite rare."

"But they only want...our skins." She was having less trouble dealing with that now, for some reason. After being told that your great-whatever-grandfather married a seal-woman, whatever that meant in terms of genetics, the idea that someone would want to kill and skin you seemed almost...natural.

Almost. But still deeply disturbing, and Beth wasn't sure how much more disturbing she could take right now. So because asking more questions would mean more answers, she accepted his incomplete answer. For now.

The motel room they got was… Beth looked around. *Dinky* was the word she was looking for. But it had two double beds and a shower that was reasonably clean, and towels that were thin but likewise clean, and they didn't ask for any identification when the two of them showed up and paid in cash.

The clerk also managed not to leer, insinuate or otherwise be suggestive at the two of them checking in midday without any luggage. Beth appreciated that. She felt worn-thin enough without having to deal with sexual innuendo from a stranger.

Bad enough the moment they got into the room Dylan had disappeared into the bathroom, and the sound of the shower had started up. Immediately visions of his body, wet and slick again, but this time warm and soapy, filled her brain. Did he soap up briskly, she wondered? Or was he the slow type, making sure every inch was lathered?

"Oh, God…enough," she moaned, and fell back onto her bed with a heavy thump. She was running for her life with a crazy man, everything she thought she knew about her family, about herself, thrown into disarray, and all she could think about was her libido?

Yes, apparently.

That settled, she took a look around. Clean, and

dinky, and not exactly high-end. The headboard was nailed to the wall, as were the cheaply framed prints and the mirror over the desk. The television was bolted to a heavy wall-mounted arm, like the ones found in hospitals.

And the bedspread was of some fabric that itched against her skin. Or maybe it was her skin that was itching. She should have thought to buy moisturizer when they were at Target. She wondered if Dylan had dry skin, too, if that was a selkie thing, or a human thing, or just a Beth thing.

"You're as crazy as he is. This guy comes to town, gets washed up onshore, says he came looking specifically for you, even though he's never even heard of you or seen you before, people start shooting at you, then he tells you your granda-times-whatever was a seal-whatever, which makes you one, and that there are people who want your skin and you've got to run, now. And you believe him! You go along with him! And you still want to jump his bones!

"You're insane, Elizabeth Havelock. Clearly, incurably, stupidly insane."

She let the sound of the words die down in the empty room and wondered idly if there was anything about the shooting on the local news. Had anyone even noticed she was gone? Unlikely—she had been holed up all week, avoiding everyone; more likely people would notice when *Dylan* didn't appear somewhere.

A sad comment on her life, she supposed, and

decided that she really didn't care if they were on the news or not. She didn't think anyone was going to cover open season on selkies, not unless someone was coming after them with clubs and...ugh.

The bathroom door opened, and a waft of warm steam came into the room. Beth rolled over on the bed and started to ask, "Why do they want..."

Her mouth dried and she forgot what she was going to ask. She forgot everything, in fact, down to her name and how to breathe.

"Oh my god, where did you get that?"

That wasn't the reaction he was expecting, based on his expression, but Beth was too horrified to care. Her eyes hadn't exactly skipped anything, but the raw red scar running down the inside of his thigh had all—all right, most—of her attention right now.

He followed her gaze down and shrugged. "Barracuda. Nasty beasts. Decided to take a chunk out of me. I objected. I won."

He waited a beat, then gently echoed her earlier words to him. "You're staring at me."

She choked on a totally inappropriate gurgle of laughter. "You're naked. Specifically, you walked out of there naked. Would you rather I didn't look?"

She expected a comeback to that, some comment or come-on. Instead, he...blushed.

"I know how to do this among my own kind. But..." He stumbled for words and swallowed hard, almost as though he was angry. "You're not human. But you are. I don't know how to do this."

His uncertainty, matched with the passion in his eyes, was irresistible. She gave up trying to resist. If this was crazy, well then she was crazy. They should, as the saying went, be crazy together.

"I'm a woman," she said, stepping closer to him. Her nostrils flared at the scent rising up off him. Clean skin, warm from the shower, and soapy, yes, but musky, too. Salt and musk, and she licked her lips, already anticipating what that toned flesh would taste like, once she put her mouth to it. Would it be like her dreams?

He groaned, and she was taken by surprise at how fast he moved, closing the short distance between them and backing her against the nearest of the two beds, scooping her up at the knees and placing her on the coverlet before she could do more than draw a surprised breath.

"Beth. Elizabeth. My Elizabeth." He stood over her, magnificently naked, and her gaze slid from his face down past his smooth, strong chest, his muscled stomach, to the erection rising quite proudly from the sparse curls at his groin. "You're mine."

"Hah. I'm *mine,*" she told him, not quite ready to be swept away into this whole "mate" thing just yet, but wanting him to stop talking and get on the bed with her already. "But I play well with others."

"I'm not playing," he said, and as fast as that he was on top of her, his hands on her shoulders, pushing her deep into the mattress, his bare leg caught between her denim-clad ones, pushing them apart at the knee, arranging her into a position to his liking, less helpless than inviting. Not that it took much doing; the moment he was distracted with undoing the snap of her new jeans, Beth snaked her arms around his neck and gave in to the impulse she had been fighting all day and then some, to touch her lips to his.

The moment she did that, he let out a moan deep in his throat, his fingers fumbling, and a touch wasn't enough. Her mouth claimed his, tongue dipping inside to discover that he did, as expected, taste of warm salt and sea spray, and something green that she couldn't identify, but immediately wanted more of. Her dream, all of her dreams recently, only better. Real. Her tongue ran over the flat of his teeth as his mouth opened, delving farther, trying to taste every inch before the need to breathe made her pull back slightly.

He had managed to unsnap her jeans while she was busy, and she was impatient to get out of the clothing, sweating and needing to feel the cooler air on her flesh, feel *him* on her flesh. She lifted her hips to help him, and he slid the fabric down slightly, shifting so that he was practically kneeling over her, on top of her. His one hand was still on her shoulder, holding her down, and in another place and with any other man she would have been uneasy at the expression on his face, the one that suggested that for all of her brave words, he intended nothing less than to consume and possess her.

If so, she knew somehow that she would also

consume and possess *him*. Unlike any man she had ever been with before, he was not holding back or building barriers even as the clothing was coming off. Everything he was, everything he could ever be, he was offering up to her. That this was…sex, yes, but more. More than a single night of on-the-lam passion, or mere physical desire. It wasn't even only love, impossible though that might be, so quickly. It was belonging. It was…acceptance.

And, honestly, she didn't care about any of that. She just wanted him inside her, moving rough and strong and sending her into oblivion. Everything else, everything, could wait until tomorrow.

His free hand slid under the waistband, fingers searching under the cotton of her panties. She had a moment's regret it wasn't something sexier, silkier, but all that was forgotten the moment his first searching finger found her own curls, slipping into the wet folds with only the slightest resistance.

"Mine," he said, and moved another finger inside her, twisting his wrist somehow so that she cried out, not quite ready to come but closer than she could have believed possible, so quickly.

"Am not," she denied, gritting her teeth as she joined in the game, resisting even as she welcomed him into her body and ached for more. Her fingers clutched at the bedspread, then reached instead for him, the warm length she could feel pressing against her thigh.

He tried to evade her, but she was quick, and he was distracted and hampered by the muscles clenching around his own fingers. Her hand closed around the thick flesh, sliding along the silky skin, letting her grip pulse, loose and then tight, in time with the beat of his pulse. She wasn't trying to make him come; the angle wasn't right, the time wasn't right. But her hand was marking him, the same way his was marking her.

"More," he growled. "More, now." His hand pulled out of her and she almost whimpered at the loss, but then her jeans were pulled off her legs entirely, the plain cotton underwear following them onto the cheap carpet. He slid his hands under her sweatshirt, discovering that she had abandoned the still-damp bra when she changed clothing. Another deep growl rose from his throat, and he cupped her breasts, thumbs stroking the tips before he bent his head to nuzzle them through the fabric. It tickled, but she had no desire anymore to giggle. He tugged the garment up and over her head, swearing as it got caught somewhere between her chin and nose. With her help it was quickly untangled, and he tossed it to join her jeans and underwear on the carpet.

"Smooth move," she teased him, reaching to stroke the side of his face to show that she was only teasing. She didn't want smooth. She wanted *him*.

"Miles out in the sea, never hearing your name or knowing your voice, I knew you," he said, kneeling between her legs and urging her to rise, meeting him halfway. Her thighs rested on his, his cock resting against her stomach. "I couldn't describe your face, but I knew how you would feel. Like this.

Did you feel me coming for you? Were you waiting for me, that night on the beach?"

She hadn't been. She hadn't known him, hadn't dreamed of him, hadn't imagined anything impossible like this. Not until she touched him. Her practical, land-born mind wouldn't accept it, even now.

But if he was right, if he wasn't crazy, there was a part of her that had known. Had rejected anything and everything else. Had been waiting, all this time.

"You came to find me. Now you've found me." She wiggled a little, deliberately, and looked directly into his dark eyes. "You going to talk all night, or—"

The rest of that sentence went unspoken, replaced by a sharp, satisfied gasp as he grabbed her by the hips and lifted her, sliding into her without hesitation.

Their chests pressed against each other, slick skin to skin, and their breathing, ragged, slowly evened out as they both adjusted to the feeling. "Mine," he said softly, so soft she barely heard him, the words soft against her neck as she started to rock, and his fingers tightened enough on her hips that she knew it would leave a bruise.

He might be crazy, in which case so was she. He might not be human, and if so, then she wasn't entirely, either. None of that mattered right now, in this place. Nothing but the two of them existed, as she felt the restlessness that had dogged her all spring build into another kind of tension altogether.

"Elizabeth…" Nobody except Ben called her by

her full name anymore. It should have sounded stilted, silly, considering their intimacy. Instead, it was sexy, seductive.... Her hands twined around his neck, curling into his hair, and she pulled him to her for another kiss. He nipped at her lips, then opened to her, allowing her tongue access once more even as he took over the motion of their lower bodies, rising and lowering her onto himself in an increasingly frantic pace, chanting under his breath. "My mate. Mine. *Mine*."

Liquid heat washed through her, starting with the muscles of her vagina and spreading down her legs and up her spine, until Beth thought she might have melted from the onslaught. She shuddered, and Dylan surged once more in response, an inarticulate grunt replacing her name as he followed her into satisfaction, each of them intent on their own selfish completion.

They rested in that upright embrace for a moment, and then began the somewhat sticky process of disentanglement. Beth felt a physical ache when his now-soft member slid from her, but then he lay down on the bed and pulled her to him, spooning comfortably with her back against his chest, his arms wrapped around her waist.

"Selkies," she said drowsily, just trying the word out.

"Seal-kin," he corrected her.

"Tomatoh, tomatoe. And these Hunters...want our skins."

"Yes."

"Why?"

He didn't hesitate this time. "My skin is magic."

"Magic." She could hear the skepticism in her voice and winced.

"For lack of a better term...yes."

She sighed and shifted to a more comfortable position within his hold. At this point, she wasn't able to argue how impossible that was. "We're in a lot of trouble, aren't we?" she asked.

"Yeah," he said, his breath warm on the side of her neck. And somehow, crazy on top of crazy, that agreement allowed her to sleep.

Unlike Beth, Dylan could not immediately find refuge in slumber. Instead, he stayed awake all night, listening to his mate breathe gently. Seal-kin weren't warriors. They were sailors, fisherfolk. Playful, not aggressive. Yet, feeling this woman snuggle up against his shoulder, stroking the soft strands of her hair, he understood the overwhelming need to defend, to protect. Even more than before, when he would have died to protect her, he knew now that he would kill to ensure her safety. Kill, without hesitation, anyone who threatened her.

And so the hours passed and the sun reappeared, and he did not sleep, trying to come up with a plan to save her, and keep them both free.

Chapter 9

Beth woke the next morning, still sleeping on top of the itchy—if now rumpled—coverlet, and found her hand reaching out to the space beside her. She was alone. The bed next to her was still warm, but the entire room was warm, so that didn't prove anything.

Normally, she would expect the memory of the previous night—hell, the previous twenty-four hours!—to make her cringe. She wasn't the kind of woman who *did* all that. Especially when "all that" included, well, all that.

Instead, she stretched, toes pointed and arms over her head, the full length of the bed, feeling every muscle in her body bitch and moan about being abused. Get shot at. Swim several miles.

Paddle same in a canoe. Walk along a dirt road, and then have mind-blowing sex. If that wasn't an Olympic-level pentathlon, she didn't know what was.

And it all seemed perfectly normal. That was the only thing really bothering her—how calmly she was taking all this. Why wasn't she freaking out? She should be freaking out. She should be *completely* freaking out. Her entire world had not only been turned upside down and beaten like a piñata, but a lucky shot had also broken it into pieces and scattered her all over the floor.

Despite that, she felt…relaxed. All right, some of that was the sex, which was exactly what the doctor had ordered. But it was more than physical, and deeper than letting off stress. Something had changed, something serious, and she had changed with it.

A wave breaking, taking her down but not drowning her. Green and blue, ribbons of shadows falling over her face…

The image came and went, barely registering. Sitting up cross-legged, still naked, on the bed, Beth went over her mental checklist.

Spring comes, and brings with it a bad, bad case of the restless twitches.

A man washes ashore down the street from her home—naked. No identification, no boat, no cash, no nothing.

That man, now clothed and named, chases after her relentlessly, with no provocation on her part.

She is drawn to the guy—admitting it now was

much easier—and resents the totally illogical attraction, making her be even more stubborn.

They are shot at by people who knew who he was, and were looking for him.

He probably saves her life. Even if he was the one who put her in danger in the first place.

He is—according to him—a selkie, or seal-kin. And so is she.

Even if he is a nutcase, that doesn't make the equally crazy people with guns go away. And she has a bad feeling he's not a nutcase.

They need to find a way to stop the crazy people with guns.

She really wants to throw him down on the bed and screw him senseless again. And then again just to make sure.

Selkie-boy is currently AWOL, so she could get neither answers nor nooky.

She was starving.

Beth Havelock was a sensible woman. Once she faced facts, she dealt with them. "Clothes, then food, then a plan," she decided. "And a shower before everything else, because, uck." Dylan had gotten his shower yesterday, and then unfairly distracted her before she could take her turn. And where was the man, anyway? The bathroom was empty when she walked into it, and unless he was hiding in the room's very small closet…

The thought came, unbidden, that he had left her. Walked out and left her there, alone, without a word of explanation. She stopped, her hand on the shower faucet, and thought about it.

"Maybe," she decided. He had appeared out of nowhere, without warning; he might leave just as suddenly. But she didn't think so.

Mine, he had said, his hands full of her hair, his legs tangled with hers. She got the feeling he didn't say things that he didn't mean. Not that way, anyway.

And if she was his... Was he, then, hers?

She thought about that for a while, luxuriating in the sensation as warm water touched her skin, when she heard the bathroom door open.

"Beth?"

"No, it's someone else who came in and decided to take a shower while she was there." She wasn't usually such a wiseass; it just fell out of her mouth because, really, who else did he think it could be? Her nose twitched; he was carrying something that smelled *incredible.* "Tell me that crinkling noise I hear is a bag containing something greasy and egg-filled, and all is forgiven."

The cheap shower curtain moved, and a bag with a familiar logo appeared briefly. "Eggy and greasy, as requested."

"Oh, thank God. Gimme two minutes."

A low chuckle that warmed her even more than the water was his response, even as the bag disappeared and the curtain fell back into place. "Don't rush, you need the time under water. I promise not to eat yours before you're done."

The door closed before she realized what he had said. *You need the time under water.* She looked down at her skin and started to laugh. That answered that, then. Made perfect sense, really. Seals lived in the water. She guessed seal-kin did, too. Apparently her mother had been right; long showers and even longer baths were a family trait after all.

The smell of the egg and bacon sandwiches was making Dylan's mouth water, but he was good and only ate his own. They had burned through a lot of calories yesterday, and dinner seemed a long time ago. She needed food to recuperate, and to keep her strength up for whatever the next wave brought.

Traditionally a male looking to prove his worth as a mate would bring the freshest fish of the day, proving his ability to provide, and then cook it up to prove that he wasn't totally helpless. He had always assumed that second part was his mother's addition to the ritual—he knew that he had gotten spoiled by his many sisters, and his mother felt the need to counteract that—but it was a good tradition.

Buying a sack of fast food didn't seem to be quite on the same level as fishing, frying and serving, but you did what you could under the circumstances. Some day he'd do it properly. First, they had to avoid the Hunters.

"Hey."

He turned to see Elizabeth come out of the bathroom. Unlike him, she had wrapped a towel around her body, but it was short enough to leave nothing to the imagination. Not that he needed his imagination. His eyes had seen everything, his hands had

touched everything, his mouth had tasted everything.

He wanted to taste her again, and to hell with
breakfast, plans, anything except making her his
own. Her legs were muscled and firm, her hips
sweetly rounded under the towel, her breasts, the
towel knotted between them, firm and pale, and the
tips, he knew, were deep rose and sweet to suckle.

"We need a plan." She moved with assurance to
the rickety table and grabbed the bag, pulling the
sandwich out and barely pausing to unwrap it before eating. His gaze rose to her face, watching her
mouth move, her throat swallow, and he had to
force himself to concentrate on her words. He
couldn't afford to be so caught up in rut that he
became useless. Not until they were safe. Then he
could, they could…oh, the things they could do….

"These Hunters. They're not going to give up?"

He shook his head, letting go of the fantasy for a
moment. "I doubt it. We're worth too much money
to them. Once they locate one of us…" The thought
was enough to distract him from his libido—and the
fact that she was eating all the hash browns, her even
white teeth tearing apart the bites with obvious relish.

She swallowed and wiped her mouth with a
napkin. "Why? You said they want our skins, but
you never said why. Not that I want details, particularly, because it's seriously not something I want
to think about, but…assuming everything else is
true, which I am for lack of anything else to believe,
what makes our skins worth having?"

That was the question he hadn't wanted to answer. Trust Beth, his Elizabeth, to ask it.

"That bad, huh?" she asked when he didn't respond right away. She put down the last bite of her egg sandwich and reached for the coffee. Her skin was so pale, her hair slicked against her scalp the way it had been in the ocean, but this time smelling of shampoo, not salt.

Awareness kicked him in the gut. She should have been safe in her house. She would have been safe in her house, her ancestry hidden, if he hadn't come for her. This was all his fault. Guilt and regret, unaccustomed and unfamiliar, rose in his gullet, making him want to rid himself of breakfast as though that would evict responsibility, as well.

She fortified herself with caffeine, and then tilted her head, looking at him. "Tell me. You've told me everything else—tell me that last thing. I mean, being skinned is pretty much as bad as it gets, right? So what…what do they do with them? The skins."

He felt sick, breakfast suddenly a greasy weight in his aching stomach even as the guilt literally choked him. She had asked. He had to tell her. Nathan had been right; his Elizabeth wasn't the sort to run or hide. "I told you that seal-kin were human once, before they…changed. The longer they lived with the cousins, adapted to life in the sea. Learned to speak with the colonies, formed their own… And they changed in more drastic ways, too."

"Drastic." She frowned, and then he saw sudden comprehension come into her eyes. "Selkies…they can take seal form, as well as human. According to the legends. Right?" She didn't wait for him to respond, but stood up and started to pace the small hotel room. Her towel slipped, and she tightened it over her breasts absently, not quite as comfortable with nudity as he was. "You...didn't have a boat, did you? When you first showed up. God, I'm a moron. You swam. In seal-form. Like you did yesterday, didn't you? That was you." She seemed to suddenly realize that she was rambling. "But your skin...where is it?"

His lips twitched, trying to hold back a totally inappropriate smile. His mate was sexy, beautiful *and* smart. She was going to make his life...challenging. Amazing. "I'm wearing it. The legends say that seal-kin have a seal-skin they put on to change form, that if you steal one skin, they—we—are trapped in the other form. Legend's not quite right. There's no second skin. Just us. Just two forms in one body."

"So they can't steal it to keep you from changing... But how do you change?" She was confused again, trying to work the puzzle out in a logical fashion.

"They steal it, just not the way the stories claim. It's not discarded on a beach somewhere, or folded up while we swim, or anything neat or pretty like that. The change, the ability...it's *in* our skins. Genetic. Seal-kin can change form, human to seal, passed down parent to child. But when the skin is placed around a true human... They can change, too. Not to seal, but to another human."

"So anyone who had a seal-kin skin…" She still wasn't quite getting it, not yet. Her mind was so practical, it hadn't quite made the jump to the wonder of what they were, just yet.

"Could change form to whatever he or she wished. One time only, change their size, shape, color…everything except their gender." And here was the truth of the matter. The reason the Hunters chased them so fanatically, the reason why a selkie's life was worth more than gold, so long as his—or her—skin was intact. "Can you imagine how much money that goes for, among humans who wish desperately to change their form entirely? To become another person, completely and seamlessly? What someone—criminals—might do to get their hands on that? On us?"

She shuddered. "But if it's part of you, how could the Hunters take it?"

"With a knife," he said bluntly. "A flensing knife, and a scraper, and a sturdy rope to hold us down, because the skin must be taken while we live, or it becomes useless."

She understood now; he could see it in her eyes, in the way her body seemed to close in on itself. He wanted to comfort her, to assure her that she would always be safe, that he would die to protect her, but he wouldn't lie to her. He would die if needed, but that alone would not make her safe. Not anymore. She needed to know all of it, to protect herself, as well.

"That's why they chase us. Why they need to be

sure what we are before they move. Why they will
never stop, once they are sure." He paused, not
wanting to kill the last light left in her eyes, but
having no choice. Not if it would keep her alert and
alive. "You can't go home. They'll be waiting. If
you had any family left—"

"I don't."

He had known that her parents were dead, that
she was an only child. The gossip he had encour-
aged had told him that much. The flat tone of her
voice, the matching flatness in her eyes, warned
him that there was more to it than that, and he
yearned to take her into his arms, to kiss the lines
between her forehead away and reassure her that she
did, now. That she had him, and his sisters and
brother, his parents and their siblings…an entire
colony who would welcome her home, to a home
that was hers by right, not just because he had
chosen her. But he said none of that, because he
didn't know if he would be able to follow through
on that promise. He couldn't go home, either, not
while these Hunters followed them. He couldn't
risk it.

"You do, though," she said. He had spoken
briefly of them, the night before, whispers of siblings, and parents. Of a colony, an island village
entirely made up of seal-kin and sea-cousins, of
fishermen and sailors, traders and the occasional
craftsman, living off the sea as much as they could,
trading with the human world for what they could
not make or harvest. He could see them becoming

real to her, where before they had been merely stories, other people in someone else's life.

"They're safe," he said. "They know the danger, and the Hunters don't know how to find them."

"So long as you don't lead them back there." She had followed his thoughts, or jumped to the conclusion herself, he didn't know. She was smart, she understood all the risks now. The very real danger they were in, not just them, but anyone they turned to. His kin, for the sake of what they were, and her friends, for their ignorance.

The lines in her forehead got deeper, and he gave in to the temptation to touch them, smoothing them out with his fingers, then standing up and moving away from her and the distraction she offered.

"Yes. We have to…stay away from them. From everyone. We have to shake the Hunters off our trail somehow." That was the right thing to do, lead danger away from the colony. His sister's children, his cousins, his kin. That obligation rose in him, as hot and strong as the need for his mate. Seals and their kin might not be warriors, but they were protective as hell.

"Okay." She looked up at him expectantly. "How? Let's do it, and then we can get back to our lives. I left a client in the middle of a project, and he's going to be significantly pissed about it."

He blinked, astonished that she could understand so much and still be oblivious to the basic fact, and spoke without thinking. "You're not going back."

He said it so calmly, it took her a second to

realize what he had said. Even then, it took her another minute to react.

"Excuse me?"

He heard the tone in her voice, but couldn't quite identify it. Irritation, perhaps. Or astonishment.

"You may be fabulous in the sack, Dylan," she went on, "and yeah, I admit we got something going even more than that, but my life is my own and you don't get any say over it."

Rage. That was the tone. He opened his mouth to protest, then decided the hell with it. Might as well be speared for a shark as a stingray, then.

"You're my mate. Or, will be, soon." You didn't win a mate just with one night and a meal. Not a mate worth having, anyway, and he already knew she was that. He rushed out with the rest of it before his nerve failed him—or she killed him. "And you would be easy prey to them, alone." He would not allow that.

All thoughts of the Hunters went out of her head with an almost audible whoosh, and she started to splutter at him. "You…arrogant, overinflated, high-handed, son of a…"

Despite himself and the seriousness of the situation, Dylan grinned. The shorter hair on the top of her head was sticking up, and her eyes were rounded and bright with temper. If he hadn't known she was seal-kin before, the temper would have been a giveaway. Selkie women were notorious for their short fuses, and a male learned quickly what was real and what was merely blowing off steam.

She was seriously angry. But not at him. He could feel that through their newly forged bond, the same way he had identified the rage in the first place. It was anger at the universe, and fates. But if he didn't defuse her, and soon, he might lose her trust anyway, just when he needed it.

She had to trust him, or she might do something foolish and get herself killed. And that might kill him.

"It's not how I wanted to do this," he admitted, concentrating on allowing his regret and ruefulness to show, to reach her through that tenuous bond. "If I could have… If I had *thought* it through, I would have done everything differently."

"Dinner and dancing?" Her hair was still ruffled, but the spark was tempered by a smidge of humor now. Still angry, still churning, but not so fierce, so misdirected.

"Maybe not dancing. But I would have wooed you. Shown you that I was worthy."

She crossed her arms over her chest and raised both eyebrows at him. "Show me now. Get us out of this. How do we stop these Hunters?"

His entire body ached to hold her, to show her off to the entire colony as his. He wanted, more than anything, to impress her. "We don't. We can't." He shook his head, aware of the odds against them. "Traditionally we evaded them, avoided them. Stayed underwater until they decided they were wrong, or that we weren't coming back." And then the colony moved, finding a new home somewhere safer.

"You mean run away. Or swim away." She was furious again, suddenly, and this time it was directed at him. He didn't understand why.

"And what then?" she asked. "Because that woman? She didn't strike me as the type to just go 'oh, well' and walk away. Or maybe she will—and come back to find someone else the next time. Maybe someone like me, who doesn't know what they are until it's too late."

He loved her passion, the fierce protectiveness that was coming to the fore, but it frightened him, too. Frightened him for her, for what it might lead her into. "You'd rather end up draped over some criminal's shoulders? Have your flesh cooling in some dump somewhere while he or she lives the good life at your expense?" Just the thought of it sickened him. The Hunters wouldn't stop to ask if she was a shifter or not, if they suspected she was seal-kin. He had just found her. How could he lose her?

"They need to be stopped!" She glared at him, as though the Hunters were all his fault, as though he had called them into being and then refused to take responsibility, and then she turned away, stalking to the other side of the room as though even looking at him was too much to handle now.

He was angry now, too. Angry at that very fierceness he had just admired in her, angry at her innocence in the heart of evil. "How do you stop a shark, Beth? They swim, they kill, they eat. The Hunters hunt. They hunt us. It's what they do."

She turned to face him, her eyes wide and the

pupils dilated. "If you hit a shark on the nose hard enough, it leaves you alone. Isn't that true?"

"Unless it's really hungry. Hunters are really hungry. We bring them too much money and power for them to back off."

She stopped, stepped away, swearing under her breath. He studied the carpet, waiting, while she muttered, moving around the room. It took a few minutes, and the tension in her was making him feel ill in a way he had never experienced before, his stomach tight and roiling like a storm. If her getting riled up made him this unhappy, he was going to have to spend the rest of his life either making sure she stayed calm, or hiding with the seal-kin until it passed.

He tried to think about the Hunters. They had been around for so many generations, were such a constant threat to the seal-kin, it seemed that the only thing to do was avoid them, the same way you tried to keep away from sharks. Sharks. Natural predators. Top of the food chain. Hunters weren't top of their food chain. What could warn them off a Hunt? What was above them in the food chain? What could scare them, and yet not threaten his people, as well?

Then Beth stopped muttering and looked back at him. The gleam in her eye was still there, but it had a different feel to it. A sharper, more focused glint.

She had calmed herself down. How? The answer came to him easily. She had a plan. From the way she was looking at him, it didn't involve hiding. The fear and queasiness was still in him, but it was tempered by a surge of anticipation. Oh, he had found himself a proper mate, he had. Life would certainly never be dull, assuming they survived.

"Beth. My Elizabeth." He had a feeling his own eyes had a corresponding glint in them. "What are you thinking?"

She shook her head, and he wasn't sure if she was denying that she was thinking, or just not ready to verbalize it.

"Tell me." He patted the bed and, when she sat down, pulled up the sole chair in the room and perched opposite her, their knees touching. "Tell me what you're thinking. Let me help work it out."

Beth lifted her hazel eyes to his, and, hesitantly, started to talk.

"You said it was all about money, to them. How much they could make."

He nodded. "From what we have learned over the years, from what we've seen, they're not bigots or cruel or sadists. Just…business folk. Everything they've ever done… I don't think they think of us as people. Just product."

She shuddered, but her words gained strength and confidence as she went on.

"That's what I thought. That's good. I mean, it's bad, but it's a weakness. For them. We can use it against them, I think."

She continued talking, and Dylan felt his pulse race with more than desire, her ideas meshing with his own thoughts, his words interspersing with hers until, between the two of them, a plan began to form.

Chapter 10

The way Dylan's ideas meshed with hers was a little disconcerting, and his utter faith in her was nice but disconcerting as well, like having a piece of cloth and suddenly being expected to wave a hand and have it become a dress.

Beth hadn't always been a planner—as a kid, she'd pretty much taken things on faith, the way kids do. After her parents and cousin died, Ben and Glory had showed her how having something always in mind gave you a thing to focus on, to build on. It was comfort, in situations where there was no possible comfort, and she discovered that things tended to go more smoothly when you had an idea of what you had to do, and what you needed to do

it. Like cooking, Ben said, it was easier to improvise a dish if you already had everything in the
pantry.

"So." She was thinking out loud the way he had
told her to, trying to mentally inventory their pantry,
as it were. "What do we have to work with? Not
much. Selkies might be able to change their shapes
with a wave of a hand…fin? Flipper? But unless
you're holding out on me, I haven't seen any sign
that you can work anything else with your…"

Say it, she prodded herself when her mind
balked at the word. Here, in this room, in front of
him, at least, say it. What's he going to do, laugh at
you? "With your magic."

Oh, God. She said it. She had really said it. For
a moment, finally, she freaked. The world spun and
rolled out of control, and she thought she was going
to start hyperventilating. Then Dylan touched her
hand, just the tip of one finger grazing along a
knuckle, and the world settled back down and was
recognizable again. Just like that.

"Well, I can sing up a boat," he reminded her.
"Although that's more…" He stopped, clearly
trying to think of how to explain it. "That's more
like encouraging the waves to bring me something
useful, than calling for a specific thing. You cast out
the request, and wait to see what comes."

"Wave-based fetch-and-retrieve. The selkie version of Google." He looked blank, and she shook
her head. "Never mind. So. Right now, we have a
wad of cash that isn't as large as I'd like, a folding

knife that probably qualifies as a concealed weapon in most states, by the way, and…that's about it." Brains, yeah; brains and the strong desire to live. And a half-baked plan that depended on luck and speed to work.

Against that, they were facing an organized group of trained professionals, established and well-funded, with probably the best weaponry and communications they could buy, whose sole goal seemed to be separating them from their skins, literally and—from what Dylan said and didn't say— while they were still alive.

That thought made her want to go back to bed, pull the covers over her head and not come out for anything, until this whole disaster went away.

The weight of his hand around hers, and the steady belief in his gaze, kept her where she was. It wasn't the usual "you can fix it" feeling she got from her clients, the "you're strong, I don't have to worry about you" attitude she got from Jake, or even the "we knew you could do it" approval that came off Ben and Glory when she graduated high school, and again when she graduated college. Dylan was worried, and he didn't know if they could pull this off, and he wasn't dumping it all in her lap. He was there, one hundred percent…together.

That confidence, that support, made her think it was all possible. That they might actually get out of this alive. "How many Hunters do you think are on our trail? Do they have backup? Office support? Financial resources?"

Dylan shook his head and pursed his lips in thought, trying to figure out how to translate what he knew into her terms. "We've never actually…" He shook off the old ways of thinking and waded with grim enthusiasm into the new. "They are always well armed, and well dressed enough to blend in anywhere, or to buy their way into any situation. So there must be money there. But they chase us on foot, or small boats, so not endless funds. They have a reliable information network that lets them find us, but they rarely come after an entire colony, instead picking off individuals or small groups. They find us by chance, or betrayal, not anything planned. So they probably don't have a huge number of people working for them directly. Not people they can trust with murder, anyway."

He said the word so casually it was almost difficult to match it with what they faced. Being hunted was different from being murdered, semantically. The end result was the same, though.

Beth swallowed hard on that realization. "All right. Good. Or, at least, better than it could have been. I had this image of, God, I don't know, some multinational conglomerate coming after us. If it's smaller, limited, it's manageable. They have limits. We just have to find them, use them.

"And how the hell do you go about recruiting someone for that kind of a job?" she wondered, going off on a tangent. "First to convince someone selkies exist, and then to convince them to club them over the head and skin them… Tough, that."

She was having enough trouble dealing with it herself, and it was her life at stake.

"In these days, yes. It used to be easier, I suspect." Dylan made a face that would have looked better on a five-year-old being offered Brussels sprouts. "The more brutal the world, the more people are willing to believe in the supernatural, the unexplainable, the *different*."

The truth of that was in front of her: two weeks ago the thought that her family wasn't…what she had thought, would have just made her laugh. Getting shot, and chased…your boundaries got expanded, all right.

"How long… Are there any restrictions on how long you can be out of the water?" She felt silly asking, but then, she knew damn-all about selkies except what he had told her, and she was pretty sure that he had only told her the smallest portion.

"I'm not a fish," he said, a little indignant. "Just like you, I prefer to take long showers—" he grinned at her "—preferably not alone, but I breathe air. No gills, remember? Or do you need a refresher course already?"

She had no idea how he did that, went from worry to lechery in the blink of an eye, and then back again, but he did, and it made the knot of worry in her chest ease slightly all over again.

Whatever happened, she wasn't alone in it. For the first time in oh, so many years, she didn't have to do it all by herself.

She kept her mind—and body—focused, but it

took effort. "Will they know that? The Hunters. They've been doing this a long time, but how much do they actually know about your people?"

Dylan settled into his chair, one leg stretched out in front of him, his elbow wedged on the arm of the chair, his chin resting on his fist. She wanted to take a photograph of him like that, frame it next to the shot of the seal in her office, for the subtle— and not so subtle—connections she could find in it. And to see if anyone else could see it, too. Did you have to know, or was it there in front of you, if you were only awake and looking? He had known what she was, and so had that woman, the leader of the Hunters. What in her face, in her body, gave her away? If they knew that, maybe they could protect themselves from discovery in the future?

"I don't know," he was saying in response to her spoken question. "Maybe. Maybe not. I mean, they know we don't have gills, but I don't know how much they actually know about *us,* other than what they need to know to hunt and…prepare us for sale."

He looked a little ill at the thought, and she suspected her skin tone wasn't much better. Best not to go there, even in theory.

He looked at the papers she had been scribbling on, puzzling out her handwriting and matching it against the map and the bus schedule he'd gotten from the motel's front desk. "So the plan is to make them think that we're hugging the coastline, and instead go inland. And then…"

She looked him straight in the eye, the green flecks shimmering even in the motel's crappy lamp-light. "After then we come back and hit them from the backside. Make them sorry they ever took this job. Make them think twice before they shoot at a selkie—at seal-kin—again."

His people might not be warriors, but she was a New Englander, a Yankee born and bred, and she damn well would defend herself and her kin!

For the first time since the beach, Beth felt op-timistic again.

Dylan, clearly, felt the same way. "You're amaz-ing, you know that?"

She blushed, and shook her head. "If it works, I'll be amazing. If not…"

If not, they would be dead. And skinned. Skinned first, still alive…oh, God, she was going to throw up.

He took her hand again, squeezing her keyboard-calloused fingers in his own much larger ones. A shiver ran through her at the contact, milder than before, as though the urgency had been muted, but was still very much there, just waiting, and the nausea faded. "It will work," he said firmly. "We'll make it work."

They checked out of the motel a few hours later, their sparse belongings packed into their knapsacks, and headed for the nearby Greyhound station. It was a small, depressing space inside a fenced-in parking lot. The building was filled with plastic seats and lined on one side with four ticket windows, only two of which were open. Beth hated it on sight, wanting nothing more than to back out the door, to go into the fresher air outside, away from the molded orange plastic and dingy gray walls. Only the fact that they had no choice kept her moving forward. That, and the fact that Dylan was already ten strides ahead of her, getting into line for one of the ticket windows.

If they had money for a plane... But they didn't. They barely had enough for this.

She adjusted the strap of her knapsack over one shoulder, checked to make sure that her sneakers were tied securely, and then, delaying tactics run through, got on the same line, making sure there were a few people between them.

Dylan bought a single ticket to Boston, leaning in at the ticket counter and flirting so outrageously with the middle-aged clerk that she was reduced to helpless giggles. It was all part of the plan, ensuring that he would be remembered if anyone asked later. Misdirection was key.

Beth, taking out her wallet and counting out the cash needed to buy two tickets inland, to Albany, felt something clench and burn deep inside her. Not jealousy, as such, because she knew that it was all a show, that he would not stray from her, but...she poked at it a little, until it unfolded enough to be recognized.

Rage. Not at Dylan, but at the innocent woman behind the counter, whose only sin was to find Dylan's charm charming.

"Seal-kin women are fierce, huh?" she said to herself, echoing Dylan's earlier words. "Buddy, you don't know half of it." The realization surprised her—she had never thought of herself as particularly passionate before: her occasionally violent springtime yearnings had always been out of character enough to be disturbing. This new side to herself should have been just as disturbing. Instead, it felt like a part of a puzzle sliding into place. It was still incomplete, holes in the entire picture, but at least now she knew that something *was* missing, and where, maybe, to find it.

She moved up in line and bought her tickets, paying in exact change and speaking as little as possible, not to avoid notice, but because she wasn't sure she trusted herself to be civil to the woman behind the screen. Her name plate said Corinda. She was a flat-faced woman, with sweet brown eyes and a mouth that seemed to smile easily, despite her depressing surroundings, and Beth felt guilty for hating her.

Hate. The difference in how she felt, all because of that casually flirting encounter—something she had planned, had *told* him to do—and her reaction to the possible actual relationship between Gena and Jake, the guy she had been dating for five years...

Beth had never understood the phrase "different as chalk and cheese" before. Now she did. The way she felt about Jake was chalk: practical, but dry. Dylan was the cheese. The thought made her smile

wickedly as she put the tickets away in her jacket
pocket. She had no cause to be jealous of Dylan...
and that certainty allowed her to enjoy the sensation of her jealousy without letting it take control—
and hopefully reap the benefits of those emotions
later.

After making sure—discreetly—that Dylan had
already left the bus station, she wandered outside
herself. A vendor was selling lunch out of a cart,
and she bought a soda and then walked down the
street to a bench where she sat, to all intents and
purposes merely enjoying the feel of the sun on her
face while killing time before her bus left. The two
buses would depart at approximately the same time,
which was why they had been chosen off the main
schedules, rather than their actual final destinations.

Ten minutes before they were due to board, Beth
tossed her now-empty soda into a nearby trash can,
picked up her knapsack and headed back into the
station, the tickets in her hand. Dylan was lounging
in the station already. She paused, admiring him
from the distance. He should have looked like any
other guy, dressed in blue jeans and a plain white
cotton tee, cheap sneakers on his feet. Should have,
but didn't. Even in repose, he looked sleek and
muscular, like... Beth stopped, shook her head. He
looked like a sleek, muscular seal, lounging on a
rock in the harbor. Totally at ease, and completely
alert at the same time.

Alert enough that when his head turned her way,
she tensed. He might have sensed her, but she got

the feeling that he was looking right past her, through her, as though she didn't exist.

Her elbows itched.

She scratched at them absently, trying to fight the urge to look over her shoulder. The bus was over there. Why wasn't he walking toward it?

danger.

Yeah, she had figured that out, thanks for the warning. She didn't know if it was Dylan's voice in her head, or simply instinct, but just as she had in the ocean, she trusted it implicitly.

Trusting it, she didn't look over her shoulder to see what he was watching so intently, but instead walked casually across the linoleum floor, past the wall of ticket windows, past the rows of molded plastic seats. Past Dylan, who was still watching the door.

He didn't react to her. She didn't react to him. But as they passed, a warm shiver ran over her exposed arms, as though he had run his palm along her skin, caressing the flesh there the way he had just that morning.

There were footsteps behind her. Heels, not sneakers: walking with a short, impatient stride. Fear pulsed in her veins, screaming at her to run, to disappear, to stay very still until the shadow of threat moved on. The conflicting urges, freeze and flee, warred in her brain, and only sheer will kept her moving at a slow, unhurried pace. She would not be spooked. She would not run, not when she had done nothing wrong. Not in this place, filled with witnesses. It was too crowded for anyone to try anything, wasn't it? Dylan had said they tended to make their attacks on isolated members, when the odds were in their favor…that didn't describe a busy bus station at all, which was why they had chosen it in the first place.

A flat male voice came over the loudspeaker, muffled words announcing the departure of the 11:14 bus to Albany, and the 11:20 bus to Boston.

That was their cue. All she had to do was go through that door and get on her bus. Easy enough, right? She shifted the strap of her backpack, forced her gut to settle down, and started—as casually as she could manage—toward the parking lot and the waiting buses.

"Police! Freeze!"

Behind her, people screamed and scattered. Beth turned to the side, finally looking back in a completely normal reaction to that shout. The first thing she saw was a man with a gun out, pointing it. Her first instinct was disbelief—was he pointing it at her?—and then horror as she realized that the muzzle was aimed directly at Dylan, who was standing very still, knapsack at his feet, hands in the air.

The second thing that she saw was the woman from the beach, several paces behind the maybe-cop, still wearing her sunglasses, even inside on an overcast day. She had changed her wardrobe to something more casual, but Beth still knew her. It had been her heels on the tile that they had heard, and reacted to.

Time was suspended, and all Beth could feel or hear was her pulse racing, pounding off the seconds until the trigger was pulled, and Dylan crashed to the floor or, worse, he was taken into custody, leaving her alone and confused. Instinct fought with desire, flee or fight, and she didn't know which urge to obey.

"I ain't going back!"

The cry came out of nowhere, as did the woman who rushed directly into the cop's path, for an instant blocking the possible trajectory of a bullet. Dylan moved smoothly, swiftly with the distraction, almost as though he had choreographed it: scooping up his pack and stepping backward, disappearing out the side door where the buses idled, waiting to leave.

The woman, a filthy, scraggly haired scarecrow of a figure, flew at the maybe-cop, swinging her handbag at him with surprising force. He ducked, trying to protect himself without actually hitting her. She had no such hesitation and went after him again, screeching at the top of her considerable lungs about how she wasn't going back, wasn't ever going back, they couldn't take her alive, she'd kill them all first.

The woman with him back-stepped, avoiding the tussle, her eyes scanning the waiting room to see where Dylan had gone. Beth took that moment to walk away, thankful for the baseball cap on her head that would hide her potentially distinctive black hair from sight.

hurry.

"Yeah, yeah, pushy male," she snapped, shouldering her way through the glass door to the parking bay. In the background she could still hear the woman screaming insults and invective, before the closing door shut them off. The diesel fumes smelled like freedom, but she didn't allow herself to relax even as she was sliding a ticket into Dylan's hand and letting him go ahead of her up the three steps into the bus. Her pulse was still beating hard, expecting a voice to shout for her to stop as she climbed those same steps, watching as the driver took her ticket and checked the destination, and then nodded for her to go ahead and find a seat.

Dylan was already seated in an aisle seat, and as she passed him, this time his hand actually did touch hers. Only a light, fleeting stroke, fingers against her palm, but it was enough to slow down her pulse to something more casually normal.

It wasn't until she had found a seat and the bus had closed its doors and pulled out of the station that she was able to relax. Once the cops—or whatever they actually were—had untangled themselves from that woman, they would discover that Dylan had bought tickets for Boston, and follow him there. She and Dylan, in the meantime, would get off at the first stop, well before Albany, and double back in time to confront the Hunters while they were off guard. If everything went the right way, if the rest of the plan went off without a hitch, they would be safe, then.

And then…

Beth didn't know what would happen then. Go back to her house, her life, her probably furious client? Run off to some isolated village with Dylan and discover…what? She still was having trouble believing—not in Dylan, but in the fact that there were others like him. Others like *her.* What if they didn't like her? What if she didn't like them?

What if, what if. Going that road would drive her mad. She supposed that she would worry about what they would do, then.

Assuming they lived long enough for it to become a problem.

Chapter 11

The voice on the other end of the phone was distinctly not happy.

"You lost them."

"Sir. Yes, sir." There was no point in denying the obvious. The crazy woman in the bus station had been too perfect a distraction; Josh should have known better than to go in with his gun already drawn, the way the displaced and out-and-out loons tended to gravitate to places like that.

"Both of them."

"Yes, sir." The male had bought a ticket to Boston, paying cash, as expected. By the time they dealt with the hysterical homeless woman, as gently as possible considering her irrational rage, the bus had pulled out already. One ticket. Was the woman still with him? If not, what had the selkie done with her? They had both been at the motel…. Had she been a hostage? That didn't follow: the selkies were passive, even when they fought. Taking a hostage was a human thing to do, a thing she would do, if threatened. She couldn't afford to project, not if she was to anticipate correctly. So why was the woman with the selkie?

If the woman hadn't drowned, and hadn't been a hostage, was her first estimation correct, that the woman was one of them, as well?

That would work out well, if true. Two skins, twice the bonus and no unfortunate witnesses.

"Follow them," her boss ordered.

"Yes, sir." Like she didn't know that. Like they weren't already gassing up the truck to head out. Like she was some newbie on her first hunt. But she had already used up any goodwill credit she had, getting the helicopter to track them in originally. She was in no position to talk back, not until she brought the damn thing in.

The connection was cut, and she put her phone away, whistling tunelessly as she looked at her watch. Three hours to Boston. They should be able to get to the station before the slower bus arrived, and be ready and waiting.

She was Hunt point. And she had lost the quarry. Responsibility was hers. And so would the praise be when they brought in not one but two prizes for auction. The thought made her smile, even through her annoyance.

"Time," she called to the rest of the team, half of whom were lounging around the van, drinking sodas and joking around, while the other half took care of personal business. "Finish up and let's go. I don't want to risk getting caught in any rush-hour traffic."

Her tone was casual. Nobody would ever know how annoyed she was. Her fingers ached, and she carefully, slowly unclenched her fingers. The joints ached, and there were small white half-moons indented into her palm.

She was not going to let these two get away from her. Not again.

They had gotten off the bus near Sagamore and gotten a room at the nearest tourist-trap motel, caring more about cheapness than aesthetic sensibility—it was cheap and tacky, but the towels were clean and it had a bed.

Beth had paced the confines of the room, worrying about what could go wrong, what she hadn't planned for, until Dylan finally forced her to stand still by the simple expedient of trapping her between his knees when she passed by him one last time. "You're thinking too much," he told her.

"What?"

"Thinking. Too much."

She stared at him as though he had lost his mind. "Dylan, we're being chased—hunted!—and you're telling me I'm—"

"Thinking too much. Yes." He placed his hands on her wrists, stilling the nervous tapping of her fingers on his thighs. "We've thought this through a dozen times. We've come up with a plan that may work or may not, but we can't do anything more about it now, can we?"

"No. No, we can't." His voice was almost hypnotic, and the way his palms were now moving slowly up and down her bare arms was definitely mesmerizing her.

"So it's time to let your wonderful brain rest a little, recharge."

"Are you suggesting that I get some sleep?"

Those sea-green eyes of hers seemed to darken with implication, and his hands slipped up, cupping the back of her head, fingers weaving into her hair as he pulled her to him. His lips brushed hers, warm breath caressing her skin as he whispered, "I didn't say a damn thing about sleep."

Her eyes had been all pupil by that point, and her response purely primal, catching his lower lip between her teeth and tugging at it, not gently, until his fingers had tightened in her thick black hair, forcing her to let go. The moment she released him, he had recaptured her mouth, tasting every bit of sweetness before moving along the sharp curve of her jaw, up to her ear, where he nipped her earlobe in turn, leaving a tiny red mark on the soft flesh.

"I was jealous, today. When you were flirting."

"Good."

She smiled against his skin, her tongue licking

at the sweat rising on his neck. He tasted good enough to warrant a second lick, and then a third. He bit a little harder, and a moan formed in her throat.

Suddenly she didn't want rough. She didn't want tumble. There was too much of that out there, waiting for them.

As though reading her mind, Dylan lay back on the bed, his hands letting go of her hair, resting on her shoulders, bringing her down with him. She fitted her length along his body, their legs tangling, arms winding around each other as clothing was shed slowly, buttons and zippers undone with care, each square inch of flesh uncovered a shared discovery.

She had slithered out of his grasp, sliding his pants down, stroking the revealed flesh of his legs, the fine dark hairs of his legs thickening around his groin, his warm, hard length rising aggressively into her touch. His skin was warm...no, hot to the touch, and pleasantly salty. Her mouth slipped down over the tip, engulfing it. She'd never really enjoyed this before, doing it more out of a sense of obligation than anything else. But this was different: the pleasure she got was Dylan's own pleasure reflected back, the satisfaction at making him groan and shift, thrust and shudder, made the physical act into a gift.

"My Elizabeth," he whispered, trying to tug her up off his shaft, reluctantly, gently, but insistently. "Come here."

She wasn't finished with him, but allowed herself to be coaxed away from the moisture-slick heft so that he could kiss her again, feeling his hands reach down and cup her ass, fitting her against him even as he rolled them both onto their sides. All four legs scissored, he slid inside her, moving gently, her hands curling up to his shoulders, his on her hips. It was gentle and smooth, like, she thought a little hazily, rocking back and forth in the waves, as the tide rolled in, and that thought made her smile even as the first stirrings of her orgasm made her toes curl and her neck arch, and Dylan shuddered, deep within her.

The sex had been for reassurance, not passion, but was no less satisfying for that, and they both fell asleep, still wrapped around each other, well before the ten-o'clock news came on.

It was too quiet. There was always noise in the morning; the clatter of wheels on the cobblestone, voices rising over the squawk of the gulls overhead, the creak and groan of ropes and planks from the ships coming into the dock or casting away. This silence was…uncanny.

They walked up from the beach, water dripping from their legs, looking for the scores of children racing down to meet them, the cats walking stiff-legged and sniffing for treats, the old men mending nets…

Nothing. No sounds. No motion, save the gentle swaying of the boats where they were tied up, waiting for use.

They walked on the cool sand, onto the wide path that led into the village, and saw no one. The single sound drew them forward, and they knew what they would see before they came to it. A pile, covered by gray-and-white winged bodies picking and pecking at the flesh. Gulls did not distinguish between fish or human flesh; it was all food to them.

"Gods be merciful," one of them said, trying to see the pile as the gulls did, and not the formless flesh of those he had once known, embraced, shared meals and laughter with.

They did what they had come to do; once the scavengers were driven away, oil was poured over the obscenity, driftwood gathered and set to it and the makeshift pyre set alight.

They did not stay to watch their kin burn. Their lives snuffed out, their souls long-fled, there was nothing left in that colony. None of the seal-kin would return, not for two generations or more. Not until the memory of the village-that-had-been was faded from the Hunters' memory, and the stink of death was gone....

Dylan opened his eyes to the darkness. He did not move, caught up still in the memory. He had not been there, on that terrible day. He knew no one who had; it had occurred five generations before, when the Hunters came in boats with sails, not motors. It was the last wholesale slaughter, the last time they were caught entirely unawares.

"Waves speed you home," he whispered into the darkness, feeling Elizabeth snuggle into his side, as though sensing his unhappy memories and seeking to comfort him even in her sleep.

Today they would set their plan in motion, using the Hunters' own assumptions to lure them, and their weaknesses to trap them. He hoped.

She turned in her sleep, one hand coming to rest on his bare shoulder, and he covered it with his own hand. The plan was a good one. It could work. It might work. But she did not know, could not truly understand what they faced. He could show her, the same way he had been shown—the shared memories of his kind. Their kind. But there was no reason for it. He already knew what her response would be. Not fear, not disgust, but anger, and even more determination to follow through with her plan.

It was their only chance, not only to survive, but also to be able to *live,* without fear or constant flight. He approved.

But still, the image lingered in his memory, brought forward the same way he had known how to act in purely human society: the bloodline ensuring that memories were shared, pooled and passed down to ensure that nothing was ever forgotten, to ensure their survival. Hunters were danger. Hunters were death.

He had never seen the skinned remains of a Hunt. But he knew intimately what they looked like. What their tortured bodies smelled like, in the funeral pyre. The taste of bitterness and regret in the throats of those who found them.

"Oh my god."

She sat up, woken not calmly, as he had been, but abruptly, painfully, kicked from her pleasant dreams by his own pained thoughts.

Dylan didn't react fast enough to catch her as she flailed, one arm thwapping him across the face. He hadn't expected her to sense anything. The connection had obviously gone deeper, faster than he had expected. Even as he took her in his arms, he found a quiet joy in that: she was bound to him now, soul as well as body. She would soon forget about her old life, and join him willingly, joyfully.

Assuming they survived long enough.

"What... They had been skinned." Her body was still shuddering. "They skinned them alive."

She had seen what was in his memory. Had felt the same things he felt; the same things those original men had felt. Had absorbed the bloodline's memory.

"I'm sorry. I'm so sorry," he apologized to her, holding her as she cried.

"They did nothing, nothing!" she cried, outraged.

"They had what the Hunters wanted. That was enough."

"Not them." She shook her head, angry at him now, that he didn't understand. "The men who found them. They burned the bodies and just left. Why didn't they do something?"

He should have known. This, Dylan thought, was why he was sent to find Beth Havelock; why of all the women, all the possible women in the world, she was his mate. Tough but loving, fair and fierce, and she thought like a human—and therefore like their human predators. She might be the saving of them all, in the end. And shorter term…he thought with pleasure that their pups would be a handful, but he was smart enough not to say that to her just yet. He already knew—and his smarting face could attest—that she had a cruel backswing.

"What would you have had them do, Elizabeth? Chase after armed men, men who are violent by nature and by choice?" He had agreed to her plan because it was the only way they could safely go home. But she had to understand what had been before, if she had any hope of understanding her heritage. "We are not warriors, my love. Poets and artists, yes. Protectors of our homes and families, yes. But not warriors. Not fighters-by-choice. The Hunters come and go, and those who survive…they don't have the taste for vengeance."

"Yeah? Well, I do." She pulled away from him, and her eyes were flat and hard. "These bastards come and think they can treat you like…like cattle. Like something to be harvested. A cash crop. War is bad enough, but to kill for money, someone who never hurt you, never did anything to you… I'd hunt them by choice. I'd pick up a gun or a club and give back as good as they tried to give me."

"You're a throwback," he said, smiling, threading his fingers through her hair, fluffing it out of pillow-head, back to its normal gloss. "Like our sailor ancestors who fought to survive. Fierce. Determined."

He thought he was saying something good, so when she looked like he had slapped her, Dylan was lost.

"Elizabeth?" His words had triggered something, something bad.

"I wasn't fierce. I was a coward." She curled up in the bed, her arms wrapped around her knees, her head bent forward so that he could no longer see her face.

He started to reach out to her, and then hesitated, not knowing the right thing to do.

"How have you ever been a coward?" He had only known her a week, but nothing in his experience suggested that she could ever be anything less than forward and brave. Hadn't she trusted him, and swum, and survived?

"I didn't want to deal. I hid. I've always hid." She took a huge gulp of air, making her shoulders heave with the effort. "I've spent the last decade hiding."

"Tell me," he said, not pushing. He had triggered this; he needed to help her through it. He owed that to her, to take on her pain, as she had shared his.

There was silence, and he thought that she had gone too far into herself, that she would not share this with him. Then she began to speak.

"My family…we always argued. My dad and me, my cousin Tal—he'd lived with us since we were kids. We were still kids. And he and my dad were going at it that day. My mom rolled with it— she was used to it. But I couldn't stand listening to them. We were going out. The four of us, into Boston for dinner. Nothing special, no occasion just…something we did, occasionally. But they were still fighting and my head hurt and I was tired of dealing with it all. So I told them I had too much work to do.

"I didn't. I was always on top of my schoolwork. My folks knew that. But they let me stay home. Tal…Tal was pissed at me. He wanted me there to distract my dad, or something, I don't know. But I didn't do it."

He already knew that she was an orphan, so there wasn't so much foreboding as a deep sense of sorrow for what she must have faced—and faced alone.

"They never came home. A truck hit them, the cops said. Slammed into the car and kept going. The car flipped over the embankment, something sparked. By the time anyone got there…the car was already in flames. Nobody got out. They never caught the guy, no idea who he was, without witnesses. Nobody was ever charged. Far as I know, they never even had a suspect."

"And you think you should have been there? You should have died?"

She almost laughed, a watery-sounding hiccup. "I don't have a death wish, no. And I don't think there was anything I could have done…but I wasn't brave, or fierce. I hid from a stupid, silly argument between two people who loved each other, because I didn't like hearing them yell. And you call me fierce?" The loathing in her voice now was thick, sticky, and directed entirely at herself.

"Very, very fierce, yes. Fierce and sad and scared

and angry at them for leaving you like that, and guilty for being angry, yes? How old were you?" he asked softly, reaching finally for her hand, relieved when she let him pry it off one knee and hold it in his own. Her fingers were cold.

"Fourteen. Tal was fifteen. We were exactly a year and a week apart. He was more my brother than a cousin. After his parents died... You look like him, a little."

"He was seal-kin, too. Like your father. A Havelock." Amazing, after so many generations, that the blood seemed to run true.

"Yeah. I guess. His mom was my dad's baby sister. She died when Tal was a baby—breast cancer. I don't remember her at all. Bob and Glory, they took care of me, were my legal guardians until I went to college, and..."

Dylan tugged at her hand, relieved when she only resisted a moment before letting him pull her into a gentle embrace, her head leaning on his shoulder. She was crying, quiet wet tears that fell onto his skin like rain on water, but her breath was slow and even. Unlike her fierce anger, her grief was contained, private. The difference fascinated him.

"I'm sorry," he murmured, knowing it wasn't enough, but hoping it helped. She felt warm and delicate in his arms, a totally different sensation from the previous night. The endless facets to her, to his reactions to her, fascinated him. It would take forever to learn them all, these sharp edges and gentle curves. He suspected that he wasn't anywhere near as complicated, and hoped she wouldn't become bored.

She hiccuped again and pulled away, wiping her eyes with the back of one hand.

"Yeah," she said. "Me, too. I don't… I must look like hell."

Her face was splotchy and her eyes were bloodshot, and her hair was matted from sleep and sweat. "Nothing a hot shower won't fix."

She almost smiled. "That was always my dad's cure, too. Your people have hot showers?"

It was a distraction, but they both needed it, so he grabbed it with both hands. "Indoor plumbing, and television, even! Although we haven't brought in cable yet. And we haven't quite figured out how to wire the village for Internet yet. We have to go to the next island over, which has Wi-Fi."

She stared at him as though she thought he was kidding.

"We don't live out on rocks with the seals," he chided her, and watched that adorable blush rise up the side of her neck again.

"I'm sorry, I guess I thought…"

He settled her more comfortably in his arms and started to spin her a picture of his home.

"Our village is, oh, twenty or twenty-five cottages. They're all cedar-sided and thatched, mostly two stories. We're not much for bright colors, mainly because they fade so fast, anyway. My mother's house is a pale blue, set up on the hill, and you can sit on the porch and watch the kin sun themselves while you drink your coffee in the morning—my mother loves her coffee."

"The seals don't come to visit?"

He laughed at the thought. "No. They have a rookery out in the harbor… When storms are really bad they sometimes come in to the shelter of the docks, but they're not house pets. You would not want them in your living room, trust me."

He thought of the feel of a kin-cousin swimming next to him, the brush of their whiskers, the stink of their breath…

"No, you definitely don't want them at the dinner table."

"Are they fierce?"

"Yes. They can be." She was more seal than many seal-kin. Was the connection somehow purer in her, for the isolation? "They're predators, for all their big brown eyes and sweet manners. The old bull who taught me how to swim, he had taken on a great white shark when he was younger, had the scars to show for it."

"Did he win?"

"You go fin to fin with a shark and live to tell about it, you won."

"Good point."

Her body was relaxed again, and the tightness had left her voice. He hated to do or say anything that would ruin it, but…

"We need a weapon. Something more than that knife."

But she beat him to it. As usual.

"Do you know how to use one?"

"Oh. No." She paused. "I swing a mean softball bat, though. You?"

"I know how to use a knife. That's why I bought that one. But I've...never used it on anything other than fish."

"The late, lamented barracuda?"

"Nobody missed it a bit, trust me." If needed, could he use that curved knife on a human? On something that walked and spoke and laughed and had family?

He thought of his lovely, soft-skinned Elizabeth, scraped raw and tossed aside to bleed to death, and he knew that yes, he could use that knife, and anything else that came to hand, to defend her. Seal-kin weren't seals, but the old bull had taught him more than just swimming.

"By now they'll have torn through the Boston station and figured out I wasn't on the bus. They'll be backtracking, looking for a pair, figuring out what bus we were on, where we got off. We have to be ready when they get here."

"We will."

Together—his knowledge and hers, his skills and her determination combining to outsmart the Hunters—they might actually be able to stop them, once and for all. This group, anyway. And...maybe more. Maybe all of them, forever.

With that thought, he kissed her on the forehead, and reluctantly untangled himself in order to get out of the lumpy, too-soft bed. He already knew she would need coffee before she was ready to do anything, much less face down a pack of soulless killers. And he was craving a bacon-and-cheese sandwich.

They were going to have to start raising pigs in the village, that was all there was to it. He said that out loud, and Beth laughed. "No fast food nearby?"

"Not for an hour's swim," he admitted. "There was rumor of a Starbucks coming in, but that was just wishful thinking. We eat pretty healthy, out of necessity, although there's a pretty strong demand for processed sugar and chocolate from anyone who goes to the larger islands on a regular basis."

She watched him finish getting dressed and mentally started listing the things they would need in order to set the trap. It was simple—she was a firm believer in K.I.S.S.—but it wouldn't do to skimp on anything.

"I hope that bitch is with them," she said out loud, interrupting her own thoughts. "I really want her to go down for the count, hard."

"Fierce," he said, and this time she heard it as he meant it, as an endearment.

"Maybe. Usually in our human, American society, it's the males who are all gung ho and bloody-minded." Beth started to laugh. "I never saw myself as the Sarah Connor type." He looked confused, and she reminded herself again not to take any cultural references for granted. "Never mind. I'll introduce you to the wonders of movies later."

Cable TV. She wouldn't really miss fast food—

she didn't eat it much, either—but he expected her to live without cable?

Survive first. She echoed Ben's imagined words of advice. *Squabble over who has the higher standard of living, later.*

She got out of bed wrapping the sheet around her, and marched over to the plywood desk that was all the furniture the room offered, beyond the bed and a rickety wooden chair. "Paper. I need paper, and a pen, and a knife. Dylan, give me your knife."

It was getting easier to ignore the fact that he walked around without a stitch of clothing. All right, she admitted, not easier as such. But knowing that she could reach out and touch, run her hand down his flank, and know that the shudder that trembled through his muscle was arousal and anticipation…that knowledge took the edge off the distraction, let her file it under "later."

Beth placed the paper on the table and took up the pen. Her hand was too steady, and she scowled at it. That wasn't going to work.

"Kiss me."

Dylan's expression was priceless, caught somewhere between little-boy-astonished and grown-man-hopeful.

"Oh, just kiss me. My hands are too steady and I need them to shake."

Her explanation sounded lame the moment it came out of her mouth, but she didn't have time to regret it before Dylan was across the room, his lithe form moving almost as fast in the air as he did in the water. He was only a few inches taller than she was, which made it easy for her to simply raise her face to receive the kiss. But he surprised her—rather than swooping down on her mouth as expected, his fingers came up to stroke the side of her face from cheekbone to chin, resting lightly there as he studied her face. His eyes were shadowed, his mouth set in a tense line, and for a moment she thought that he was going to refuse her request.

Then he did swoop, fingers sliding up against her scalp, holding her head steady while he plundered her mouth. His lips were cool against hers, but his teeth were sharp as they nipped her flesh, and when she tried to protest, his tongue slipped warmly against her own, tasting, and leaving that salty green tang behind in return.

Her own hands had been resting flat-palmed on the table; now they lifted as though of their own accord, curling lightly around his forearms as though not sure if she wanted to pull him closer or push him away. His breath was hot on her face, his body inches away that might as well have been a mile, for all the contact they made; it was all fingers and lips, breath and spit.

She broke away, her knees wobbling.

"That'll do it."

She sat down rather more abruptly than planned and picked up the pen.

Help me.

Her handwriting was suitably shaky, like a woman under duress. She thought about adding more, but decided that brevity was more likely to work. They needed to bait the trap, not overact a melodrama.

"The knife?"

He hesitated, his eyes still dark and stormy as he watched her.

"Come on, we agreed. The knife."

"Let me do it."

"Can't. If they check…I'm on record." She was a regular blood donor; if anyone really wanted to make sure, they could get her records, somehow. She doubted Dylan could say the same. And if his people were as secretive as they seemed, that was how he'd want it.

This had to be one hundred percent real for it to work.

He swallowed hard, but took the knife out of the neoprene sheath and handed it to her, hilt-first. It was a lovely, dangerous thing, simple lines and sharp edges in the black plastic handle, and she didn't doubt that it could fend off anything that grabbed a leg in the watery depths.

"Be careful. It's sharp."

"I noticed."

He looked like he wanted to say something else, then thought better of it.

"Right, then."

Now her hand really was shaking, and she had the passing thought that she should have done this first, and then written the note.

"This is harder than I thought it would be," she said with grim humor. "All those warnings my mother used to give me about running with sharp objects must have actually sunk in."

He reached out as though to take the knife from her, to prevent her or to do it himself, she didn't know. Not waiting to find out, she gritted her teeth and jabbed upward.

"Ow!"

"I told you it was sharp!" he said, annoyed, and suddenly there was a towel wrapped around her hand, catching the blood that was dripping out of the slice in her palm. She tilted her hand so that a drop escaped and scattered across the note. With her unbloodied hand, she smeared it across the corner of the page.

"Keep pressure on that," he directed her. "And keep it elevated. What were you thinking? A little cut would have done the job. Humans!"

He said that word, she thought, sitting back down, like some men might say "women," and some women said "men!".

"I'm fine," she said, waving him off. "Done worse with an X-Acto blade."

He gave her a Look, but picked up the note and folded it carefully. "You really think this will work? They know you're seal-kin. You heard the Hunter on the beach—she knew."

"Yeah. Maybe. But they can't be certain. And even if they are, they're not the ones this is for. Having them wondering if I'm really a helpless victim will put them off balance." She hoped.

He glanced at the digital clock on the cheap dresser. "Almost time."

By now, the Hunters should have traced them to this town. It wouldn't take much longer for them to determine that two strangers had taken a room.

Beth pressed the towel against her palm and winced. She probably should have let Dylan nick her. He was the one with the knife-wielding experience.

Dylan, meanwhile, had put the knife back into his bag, and had dropped the bag next to hers by the door. "Might as well make that bit of stupidity useful. Come here."

He had that ordering-around voice again, but she got up with a sigh—he had gone along with her ideas, she would go along with whatever he'd thought of, too.

She came up next to him, unwrapping the towel as she went. The blood was thickening already; she had always been a quick healer but this seemed faster than normal.

"You're amazingly brave," he told her.

"I'm terrified out of my mind," she admitted.

"I know. But you're still doing this. That's—"

"Bravery, yeah, I know. I've gotten the speech before, too. I'm still terrified. If you weren't here…"

She could tell that his first reaction was to take responsibility, to take the blame. She glared at him, and he kissed the tip of her pointed nose. "I am here. I will always be here, so long as here is where you are."

It was a promise nobody could make and keep, not with one hundred percent certainty. Beth knew, with hard personal experience, that things happened, people left you, even people who loved you. But…she believed him.

He took her bleeding hand and kissed it gently, then wrapped the palm around the door handle, the weight of his hand forcing the cut to open again against the metal. She cried out, more from surprise at the sharp pain than the pain itself. "Hold it there a moment," he said, his voice muffled against her hair, barely reaching to her ear. "Spoor, in case they bring in a tracker."

Spoor. Right. "This is not how I normally spend my Saturday. Just so you know."

"I'll make it up to you," he promised with another kiss.

"Damn well better," she said, not believing it, not really, and let go of the door handle. "Let's do this."

Chapter 12

"Nine-one-one. What is your emergency?"

"Help me. Please." Beth put a little extra curl of pathos into the last word, figuring that overkill was better than coming across as too calm. Her body tensed up, and she let it. Method acting, right?

"Ma'am?" From the extra attentiveness the operator put into that word, it worked. He was convinced.

"Help me." A gasp, as though she was terrified. Not so much acting there, actually. She was scared out of her mind. Just not for reasons she could tell this nice man. "Oh, God, he's coming back. Please, help me...."

"Ma'am, who is there? Can you get away

safely?" An almost minute pause, as the operator read information off his screen, determining the exact address she was calling from, the precise location of the caller. Thank God for technology. "Ma'am, I have a squad car on its way...."

Beth dropped the phone onto the cement, hating herself for worrying the operator, and maybe taking a cop away from somewhere important, and turned to Dylan. His brown eyes were shadowed with the same regret she could feel etched into her own face. This was an emergency. It *was*.

He reached out and took her undamaged hand, drawing her away from the phone and out of the old-fashioned phone booth, amazingly still in working condition despite the overwhelming presence of cell phones everywhere. Hers was at the bottom of the ocean somewhere, probably. Or maybe ringing inside a tuna with indigestion....

One operator, and one squad car, for the greater long-term good. It wasn't as though they were in any kind of a high-crime zone, and there was a crime being committed—she was just calling the emergency in preemptively. She wasn't doing anything wrong. She kept telling herself that.

Only once out of range of the phone did Dylan speak.

"By now, whoever was cleaning up the motel room will have found the note, and seen the blood. Are you sure they'll do something?"

"No." She wasn't sure of anything right now, except that she wanted very badly to bury herself in Dylan's arms and not come out again. "But that's why I slipped the cabbie who brought us down here a twenty, too, so he'd call the cops. Or, better yet, the press." Her blood had been on that bill, too. Not intentionally, it just happened, but nice verisimilitude. A little too nice, maybe. Between that, and the way Dylan had manhandled her out of the cab... She doubted he'd ever heard of method acting, but he played the part of the maybe-kidnapper, maybe-ex-boyfriend pretty well. Only the way his hand trembled on hers, and the soft brush of his lips on the back of her neck in apology, gave him away.

There was going to be a lot of explaining required to everyone, after all this. If the cops actually showed up.

Assuming that they actually got out of this in any position to explain. She supposed someone more heroic, someone more self-sacrificing, would believe that their deaths would be worthwhile if the Hunters could be stopped, once and for all. She was pragmatic, practical and a planner. *Heroic* did not begin with *P*.

The idea wasn't to wipe the Hunters out, anyway. Being practical and pragmatic, there was no way she could create a plan, with their very limited resources, to do that. They could, though, send a message: the selkies of this territory were not easy prey any longer. That they would fight back, using modern means and modern protections.

If Hunters were all about money, then she— they—were going to hit them where the money lived.

Her hand had stopped bleeding, and was in fact nicely scabbing over. Was she healing any faster than she usually did? No, she didn't think so. Wishful thinking, maybe. Probably the cut had been bloody but not really so very deep after all.

She took Dylan's hand in her uninjured one and tugged him over to the side of the seawall, a low stone fence that ran the length of the beach, over-looking a length of sand ending with wavelets that lapped gently at the shore. It was high tide, and she could see tiny pleasure boats bobbing at anchor, and farther out, the larger fishing boats heading to shore with their catches.

This was a small harbor, catering to sailboats and small powerboats. There weren't even any day-charter boats moored here, so it was quiet and peaceful and perfect for their plan. A simple, prac-tically foolproof plan, except for the fact that so much could go wrong.

"If this doesn't work…" she started to say.

"It will work."

"If it doesn't. Hit the water. Change. Do what-ever it is you do, just get out of here."

He looked at her, his eyes even wider than before, wider and darker in disbelief. "My Eliza-beth, I won't leave you."

"Not even to save me?"

His blank look wasn't quite adorable—in fact, he looked, well, like someone had hit him in the head with a hammer. But it melted her a little anyway, because the fact that he would do anything—even something he hated to do—in order to save her was still something new and to be treasured.

"I have a presence here," she said, sitting on the wall and tugging him down with her. Their legs dangled a few inches off the sand, and the stone was cold under her ass, even through the fabric of her jeans. "I'm a citizen, I pay taxes and have friends who will raise a fuss if something happens to me, who may already have raised a fuss." They weren't counting on it, but it could only help the plan if someone—Ben and Glory, or Joyce, or Jake or anyone—had noticed that she was missing, and yelped. "That may slow the Hunters down—or, worst-case scenario, it might get them into serious trouble when my deskinned body shows up somewhere, chock-full of oh, so identifiable DNA."

She already knew, through the dream, what the Hunters did with the deskinned bodies. Their methods might have gotten more sophisticated over the years, but they were still careless, knowing the seal-kin had no recourse, no place in modern society. Her body, tossed aside, would become evidence that, combined with the note left in the hotel room, and the call to 911, might be enough to hang them, even if the main plan failed.

Oh, God. Would they charge Dylan? If he wasn't in the system at all, they'd never be able to prove he even existed, and the Hunters had to have left some trace that could be tracked. She held on to that hope, even as her brain started to run scenarios to deal with things she might have missed.

"I won't leave you," he started to say again.

"You'd force me to watch you die, first?"

It was a low blow, and she watched it land with masochistic satisfaction.

"I'll do what seems best, if it comes to that" was all he could give her, and she accepted it. If they got lucky, it wouldn't come to that.

"How long do you think we have? Before the Hunters find us, I mean."

Dylan looked up at the sky, calculating something. "An hour, maybe. Maybe not even that. We gave them the slip because we took them by surprise. But that will only have annoyed them."

"That woman seemed like the sort to get pissed off easily, yeah." Beth was amazed at how easy it was to be flip about it. She had always mocked heroines who quipped their way through danger, but obviously all those late-night movie marathons had gone deeper into her psyche than she thought. Or maybe it was just easier to be flippant than admit that you were scared.

"That woman is a barracuda," Dylan said. "I think fear turns her on. If she makes any kind of move in your direction, don't run away—charge her."

"I thought it was sharks you hit on the snout?"

"Barracudas are—"

She never got the chance to find out what he thought barracudas were—there was the distinct sound of car tires on the gravel road behind them, and he shoved her off the seawall, so that she landed on her knees on the sand below, her head below the wall and invisible from the parking lot.

"Stay down!" he ordered her.

"Is it her?"

"Hush!"

She had never taken well to being hushed. Or pushed, for that matter. She decided she would forgive him this once.

"She's here. And four goons."

Only four. There had been at least that many on the beach the first time. Either the woman hadn't called for backup, or there was backup and they were staying out of sight. Assume worst-case scenario. Where would the backup be waiting, and until when?

Beth had chosen to make their stand on Cape Cod—and this specific harbor—for a number of reasons. She knew the area reasonably well. It was easy to get to from the mainland, for one—just over the bridge and down the road. Second, it was well-populated enough that anyone planning anything illegal would have to be cautious. No meets in dark, secluded groves for this girl, no. Again, watching all those movies late at night when she was a kid was finally paying off.

And third, it wasn't her home. She agreed with Dylan on that—you didn't give them the chance to strike at the people you cared about. She knew people here, but none of them were family, and none of them had obvious ties to her. Nobody the Hunters could drag into their sick games.

"No sign of guns." Dylan was keeping a running commentary, barely moving his lips as he spoke.

"Fourth man still in the car, engine's running. No other car—unless they put us in the trunk, they're going to be doing it here."

"I bet they like the sand. It soaks up the blood, gives them a place to dump the bodies, and the tide takes care of any traces they might leave behind." She was scanning the water, making sure that no small boat was coming in toward them. All quiet.

"Yeah." He must have the same memories she did now. The shadow of that dream swept over her again, and she shuddered, a full-body quake.

His gaze raked down the long narrow driveway leading to the main road. "Where are the cops?"

"We don't want them here until something happens," she reminded him. "Otherwise— Someone's coming." She had heard the sound of tires on the gravel before he did.

"A truck. One of those little ones, with stuff on the top."

Stuff. What stuff? She risked peeking over the wall. A van, dark blue, with antenna gear on the top. "A news crew?"

She ducked below the wall, her back to the stone, and stared out at the bay. A news crew. What the hell was a news crew doing here? Was it sheer bad luck or...

"The cabbie probably got a better deal from them than the cops," she said in disgust.

"News? Television?"

"Local station, cable news. Damn it."

"That's not good?"

"Guns versus cameras? Do the math, Dylan."

"But they're human. Totally human."

"Which means they're witnesses. Damn it, we need to get them out of here!"

"Or not." He caught her shoulder before she could protest. "Think about it, Elizabeth. Media. Better than police, anyway. No guns… Coverage. Publicity."

Beth stared at him and felt a grim smile creep onto her face to match his own. He was right. Played carefully, this could work—and keep Dylan out of official view, as well.

She put her hands on the top of the wall, wincing as the grit pressed against her cut, and pushed off anyway, climbing back over the wall.

"Dylan!"

The woman in sunglasses. She was wearing jeans now, and the leather jacket, and her hair was pulled back in a braid. She looked way tougher than either one of them could handle, even without her goons. No guns visible…but one of the goons had something in his hand, something that glinted bright in the afternoon sunlight.

A knife. A large, curved knife. Beth felt the bottom of her stomach plunge into somewhere around her knees, and she wondered if she had time to throw up.

There was the sound of a door opening, and a guy got out of the driver's seat of the van, even as the side of the van slid open and a guy with a camera on his shoulder got out.

Damn. At least it looked like it was just a roving camera crew, not a hotshot reporter who would want to get up in their faces and ask exactly the questions that would get them killed.

"We still need to get them out of here alive," she muttered. A shadow fell over her, and she looked up just in time to see Dylan move forward, away from the wall and toward the newcomers.

"Dear heart, you had better be a better improviser than I am," she muttered, jumping down lightly onto the ground and following him. "Because we are so damn off-script we're not even in the same game anymore."

"Get them out of here!" Dylan heard the woman snap at her goons. He assumed that they were talking about the news crew, and doubted the goons were there to use sweet talk and logic. He didn't know exactly what he was going to do to prevent bloodshed, except that standing on the wall waiting for someone to get shot at wasn't going to help anyone, least of all them.

"Dylan." The Hunter had turned her attention back on to him. She removed her sunglasses, staring at him as though expecting her glare was enough to halt him in his tracks. "Don't do anything rash. If you come quietly, nobody else needs to get hurt."

Part of him was willing to agree. The seal-kin soul, who knew the seas were a dangerous place, that under every wave might lurk a shark, that every cliff might hide a Hunter, that every beginning has an end, heard the truth in her words. She wanted profit, not a scene. She was looking for him, not anyone else.

If he went with her, Elizabeth might escape. The innocent humans would never know how close to death they were. All it would take would be his acquiescence to what was inevitable, anyway.

don't you dare.

White-hot anger, and a sense of outrage. And then Elizabeth was striding past him, ignoring the Hunter as though she didn't even exist, walking steadily toward the news crew. "I don't know what you came here for but we really don't want a film crew around, so you might as well look for something more interesting elsewhere," she was saying. The human with the camera didn't lower his instrument, and the one with the mike in his hand almost laughed.

"It's a free parking lot, last time I checked. We can't get some footage of a lovely day on the shore?"

Apparently stubbornness wasn't reserved for seal-kin.

Goon #2 was even with Elizabeth, and the smirk on the reporter's face was fading when he saw the knife glinting in his hand. He muttered something to the cameraman, who turned and started filming the goon instead of Elizabeth, and the driver got back into the van, starting the engine again.

Dylan realized that he was spending too much time paying attention to what was happening ahead of him, and not enough behind, when rough hands grabbed his arms and forced them up behind his back, a sharp blow behind the knees forcing him down onto the sand. Goon #1 slipped a rope around his neck, and pulled it tight enough to jerk his head backward at a sharp angle: not enough to damage his spine, but the potential was there. Even if he changed, the rope would still be able to snap his neck—leaving him alive and paralyzed long enough for a skilled Hunter to remove the skin before finishing him off.

"Elizabeth." The woman called her name, and she stopped cold. Dylan's heart paused in his chest.

"Don't do anything foolish. Look behind you."

He willed her not to turn around, but she was already moving. Slowly, as though knowing what she would see. Her face, when he could see it, was cut from stone, but her eyes were anguished, even at this distance.

Please, he begged her silently. Don't do anything foolish. Don't get yourself killed. Don't make me watch you die. I want that even less than I want you to see me die.…

"Are you getting this?" the reporter asked the cameraman, who didn't even bother to reply. The camera kept filming.

Goon #2 moved, and Dylan involuntarily strained against the rope, but the knife-holder by-passed Elizabeth entirely where she stood, frozen on the gravel, and instead grabbed the reporter. The blade went up to his neck, and held there.

"I would stop filming now, if I were you," the

woman advised the cameraman, her voice almost gentle.

Yes, Dylan thought intently. The hell with the plan. Stop now. Nobody needed to die today.

"Stop and I'll kill you myself," the reporter said.

"You will already be dead," the woman said, her voice still as soft, the words as much a threat as the knife.

"Lady, I've blown deadlines before. Hasn't stopped me."

Either the reporter didn't understand or didn't care. Dylan didn't know and didn't care, either. If the woman didn't care about killing humans, the plan had failed. The news crew would die. His Elizabeth would die; even if her skin held no magic at all, they wouldn't know that until they had taken it from her, tortured her. Killed her and dumped her body.

His heart had started beating again, too fast. His gaze met Beth's, and he tried to pour his love, his regret, into that gaze. It wasn't enough. He needed to touch her, to hold her, to keep her safe. His need overwhelmed everything else, even common sense. His mate was threatened, and he was helpless.

His skin itched, feeling dry and rough.

You are not human. You are seal-kin.

The voice told him nothing he did not already know, and he would have flicked it aside, except for the images that accompanied it. Images from his childhood spent in the waves, on the rocks, sleeping with the seal-cousins, watching and learning as much from their example as from his mother's.

Seal-pups, daring their first swim. Dams, protecting the young against the bulk and occasional anger of the males. Males…swaggering with the mating urge, competing for the right to breed, both in play and seriously, giving in to the urge to survive, one way or the other…

You are seal-kin. You are not *helpless. And you do not act alone.*

Understanding grew. The reporter wasn't just risking everything for a story. He was changing the odds, the way dolphins sometimes helped others, even humans, escape sharks by distracting them, holding them off.

There was a chance that the plan could still succeed. Risky, dangerous. It meant more risk. It meant being powerful, as well. It all depended on how skilled the man holding him was—and how distracted he was by the drama in front of them. How much they could trust these reporters. And how much Dylan himself was willing to risk.

Even as Dylan thought that, he was rising, charging forward with every muscle in his body thrown into one goal. As he had hoped, the element of surprise caught his captor off guard, dragging the man off his feet even as the rope tightened around Dylan's neck.

A neck that was changing form even as he moved, as his skin rippled and flowed around him, his shadow falling away and sliding to the ground under his feet, the rope slipping over a head that could now move at angles a human neck could not, a body that was shaped and weighted so differently, the Hunter had to regroup and recapture him.

It was one thing to try to skin a helpless foe. It was another to take down an enraged, full-grown, uninjured bull seal in defense of his mate.

The bull gave the human no chance, but moved forward. Not to the side of his mate, but to the source of the threat: the woman wearing the leather coat. He wasn't large, as true bulls went, but his weight was greater than his human form, and almost entirely solid muscle. He hit her hard, his rounded head smack against her abdomen, and she went crashing against the hood of the sedan, setting off the car alarm and making two other goons tumble out, their guns drawn and ready to fire.

He kept the Hunter pinned against the car, knowing that they dared not shoot him, not now that he had changed: their only hope was to coax him back into human form, and take him hostage again.

"Dylan!"

But Beth didn't know how to change, or if she even could. He hadn't told her…there was so much that she didn't know, that he hadn't thought to tell her yet. Hadn't let himself worry about, with so much else yet to deal with…

The human mind held sway, even inside the seal-form, and he reared awkwardly up to his full height, snout-to-face with the Hunter.

She stared back at him, not an angry glare, or a frightened one, merely…a stare. All business, this one. Good. That was good.

Some of his own anger washed away in turn, giving him room to think. The human mind was in control, his possessive anger still simmering, but submissive to rational thought. The plan was changed, but it could still work. Could even work better, if he did everything right.

He risked a glance over his sloping shoulder. The two goons with guns were still there, one of them aiming at him, the other with the barrel pointed at Elizabeth. The knife-wielding goon was still holding the reporter, and the cameraman was still shooting film. The third news crew member could be seen dimly through the car window. It looked as though he had one hand on the wheel, and the other was holding a cell phone up to his ear.

He might be calling his station. He might be calling the police. For all Dylan knew, he was calling to check for the most recent sports update. It didn't matter. The unknown man had to be…not discounted, but not counted on, either.

And where the hell were the police! How dare they ignore his mate's call for help?

His Elizabeth. Her voice. She was speaking.

"What we have here," she was saying, her voice hardly trembling at all, "seems to be a bit of a standoff."

"We have the guns," one of the goons said, twisting his so that the sunlight gleamed on the barrel.

"True. But if you were going to shoot either one of us, you would have already. You roped him, and threatened someone else with the knife, so obviously damaging our skins is not on your sick—and it is really, really sick by the way—agenda."

"They want your skins? Because of seal-boy over there? Are you like that, too? Max, are you getting all of this on film?"

Even with an oversize blade to his jaw, the reporter couldn't resist asking questions. The goon holding him jerked the knife a little more tightly against the stretched-tight skin, and he finally subsided. The faint hint of human blood drifted into the air, discernible only by Dylan's hyperaware nose, and it made him shudder.

"Back off," the Hunter whispered, her words clearly meant for him alone. "Back off and I will give orders for my men to let her go. You are the one we came for—you're the only one I've recorded. Come peacefully, and nobody else need know about her."

It was tempting. It was also, he knew now, a lie. He had changed in front of witnesses. The Hunters could not allow that to remain unchecked. They operated only out of the rest of the world's ignorance.

That was what he was now depending on.

And even if he wasn't determined to bring this damned Hunter down, he had made a promise to his mate not to die. He didn't break his promises.

"Yeah, they want our skins. They're collectors." Elizabeth was speaking again, standing between knife and gunpoint as poised and calm as though she were in her own home. A home he had never seen, he realized. He didn't know her favorite colors, what she liked to eat, or even if she was a morning person or a night person, really. He knew that she hogged the pillows, that she slept on her stomach with her knees curled to the side, and that she liked to snuggle after sex....

And that he wanted the rest of his life to learn everything else.

My mate. Mine.

"They'll kill us...and you, probably, because you were in the wrong place at the wrong time." Elizabeth was still speaking in that calm voice, her gaze on the reporter, flicking occasionally to the bull seal, but never losing track of who she was speaking to.

"She's insane," the Hunter said. "We were trying to capture them peacefully, to prevent them from harming anyone else. You saw how this thing charged me, attacked me—can you imagine it in the middle of a crowded mall, losing control like that?"

"Lady, no offense, but your guy's the one with the knife to my throat. I'm not really inclined to be sympathetic to your line."

"Fucking crazy bastard," Dylan heard the cameraman whisper, in tones that were half despair and half admiration, and he felt his whiskers twitch in amusement. They were still filming. Everything was being caught on tape....

"So what now?" the reporter asked Beth. "My guy's in the van calling the cops, and they say they're already on the way, soon as the damn drawbridge comes down. But are cops really gonna help matters any, or just get us all killed that much faster?"

A good question. Dylan didn't know.

"There's only one way out of a standoff," Beth said. "Everyone backs off at the same time."

"Yeah, and why do you think we're going to do that?" Goon #3 asked, speaking for the first time.

"Because once the cops arrive, one way or the other, it's over," Beth said with calm practicality. "You can shoot everyone, and then, hey, guess what? You've got human blood on your hands. Worse, you've got cop blood on your hands. You people operate out of sight, out of belief. People may not believe in selkies, but they do believe in cop-killers. You think your bosses—you think that your *customers*—want that kind of attention? Especially attention backed up by film?"

There was a long, drawn-out second of hesitation, filled with tension like broken glass.

"Marg—"

"Shut up!" the woman snapped, and Goon #3 subsided.

"That still leaves you with the film," the woman said. She had abandoned the sweet tones, and was back to the brisk, businesslike voice she had used before on the beach, during their first confrontation. "Not that I believe anyone will trust the veracity of your…exposé, but I have no desire to be splashed over the evening news, even on a Podunk little channel such as yours. Give me the film."

"Hell, no, I won't," the cameraman began, but Elizabeth interrupted him.

"She's right. Nobody will air the film, not without a murder on it, and I think we can agree that's not the optimal way to end this? Worse, if you try to air it yourself, they'll mock you, or call you fakers. I work with digital images—I know how easy it is to fake things like this, and how hard it is to prove it's for real. All it can do is harm your career. Live, and let it go." She looked at him meaningfully, and something passed between them, some understanding that Dylan saw but wasn't part of.

The cameraman then looked to the reporter, who nodded carefully, aware of the blade still being held to his chin.

"You think maybe we could start with you not giving me so close a shave?" he asked.

The goon looked to the woman, who nodded. He lowered his arm, just enough to allow the reporter to swallow and stretch without risking his life.

"Thank you." The sarcasm was coated with a heavy hand. "Now back away, and put the shiny sharp thing away. Jesus, man, you've got guns still, if you're so insecure in your masculinity."

"Pissing them off isn't going to get you out of here intact," Beth warned him, and Dylan heard the thread of exasperation in her voice, even under the tension.

"He can't help it," the cameraman said, grinning tightly. "It's why he's still bush leagues with the rest of us, a terminal case of wiseoff."

"Let him go," the woman ordered, and the goon stepped back, releasing the reporter entirely. "And now it is your turn. Please call it off."

Beth turned to Dylan, and then looked at the Hunter. "I think maybe you need to ask him your-self. Nicely. Treating him like an inanimate object? Not going to put him in a good mood. And I hear tell that seals are kind of short-tempered."

He almost barked an objection—he had told her no such thing!—but the thought of the Hunter being forced to acknowledge him as more than a thing overrode all other considerations. He looked down at the woman, his whiskers almost in her face, and waited.

"Well?"

"Get off me. Please."

He didn't move.

"I don't think he believed you were sincere in that please."

"Jesus, now who's the wiseoff?" the reporter asked.

"Please back off, so we can get this farce over with." She gritted her teeth as she spoke, and Dylan could feel her muscles tensing up again. He wasn't sure how much further they could push it before she became dangerous again, so he shoved his weight off her—not being too careful how badly he bruised her—and moved back several yards.

"Sweetie, it might be better if you were in less…attention-garnering shape."

Dylan almost missed what she was saying, listen-ing instead to the sound of the words. She called him "sweetie." It wasn't an endearment he was used to, or one he particularly liked, but from her…it was music.

She was right, but he hated to change in front of anyone—outside of the panic of earlier, the change was a moment of exposure, and intimacy, and there was no way she could understand that yet. He barked once, hoping that she would understand, and moved carefully around the sedan, avoiding the still-open door until he felt that he was enough out of the line of sight of the humans—and the camera.

He closed his eyes and summoned his human shape back to him. If anyone had been watching, they would have seen his shadow, discarded earlier, slip along the sand as though dragged by an invisible thread, skimming back to reattach itself soundlessly to his now-human form.

The fact that he was naked now was just going to have to be dealt with—nobody had ever been able to figure out what happened to clothing during the change, or why it didn't come back with the human form. It was one of the reasons his people didn't worry too much about clothing overall, except as needed against the elements.

He stopped, lifting his head to listen, while the others kept talking. His hearing wasn't anything better than human-normal, now, without his seal-form's ability to hear vibrations, but there was something...

"Elizabeth." He stepped out from behind the car, and all conversation stopped. "The police are coming."

Now, everyone could hear the sirens.

Goon #2's gun rose again, even as the woman demanded, "The film, if you please."

"Do it," Beth ordered the cameraman, and the reporter, reluctantly, nodded. With a sigh, he lowered the camera and removed the deck, handing it over to the nearest goon.

"The purest form of a compromise," the reporter said. "Nobody's happy."

"And everyone's alive," Beth said. "I can live with that." She looked levelly at the Hunters, as though reminding them that their part of the bargain wasn't quite done yet.

"If you don't mind, we will be going now," the woman said, taking the deck from her goon and tossing it into the backseat of the sedan. The guns weren't lowered until they were tucked inside, and the doors shut, and the driver took off.

Only then did Dylan actually relax.

At that point, the cameraman shoved his now-useless camera into the back of the van and hit the top of the vehicle with an open palm. "You can come out now, you worthless coward."

The driver's-side door opened, and a young man, barely shaving age, popped out. "Because what?" he demanded indignantly, "I could do so much, out there with youse? I should get myself shot or sliced, that would make you feel so much better?"

"Yes!"

"Tough!" And he dropped back into the van and slammed his door shut.

"Let's go, man," the cameraman said, then stopped and looked at Dylan. He cracked a grin, shook his head and reached into the open side of the van, pulling out a pile of fabric. "I don't know if they'll fit, but better to be nailed by the fashion police for tacky than the real ones for indecent exposure."

Dylan thanked him for the offer, but indicated the knapsack Beth was bringing over, with the extra clothes he'd bought the other day. Thankfully he had kicked off his cheap sneakers before changing—that habit was trained into them all about the third time they had to pay to replace their own shoes—and he was able to retrieve them off the sand and slide them onto his bare feet.

"It would have been a hell of a scoop," the reporter was saying to her, sadly. "Even if nobody would have run the tape. An exposé on crazy rich people who hunt other folk for their skins? Wild, totally wild."

"You want to have fun, and help us out, too?" She turned to the cameraman. "Was I right, or was I right?"

"You were right," he said, with that tight grin back on his face, and he pulled out a small black object.

"You son of a bitch," the reporter swore. "You were taping this, too?"

The cameraman shrugged eloquently. "Remember when we lost sound last year, during the rally? They give us such crap equipment in this van, I've been running backups ever since."

"You don't have the film anymore, true," Beth said, "but you do have proof. I bet there are any number of magazines that would take the story, even without pictures. And pay for it, too."

The reporter tilted his head like a sandpiper, waiting for her to continue. She smiled at him, a sweet smile filled with mischief that Dylan could already recognize.

The cop car rolled into the parking lot, and cut the sirens the moment they realized that there was no obvious danger. Dylan, now dressed, went out to greet them, giving Elizabeth and the reporter more time to work out whatever it was she had up her sleeve.

Chapter 13

It took some quick talking, something Dylan had never really thought he was good at before, to convince the newly arrived police officers that everything was fine, no need to worry, sorry for the trouble.

The first cop out of the patrol car, a slightly overweight man with hair gone gray at his close-cropped temples, moved like an old walrus, slow and ponderous. Dylan wasn't foolish enough to underestimate him, and kept his own movements slow and unmistakable. Like a walrus, this man could do damage if he thought there was a threat. "Can I see some identification, son?" Walrus asked when Dylan ran out of steam.

Dylan moved his hand automatically to the

back pocket of his jeans, where he had been storing the money clip, before remembering that he didn't actually have any identification on him. Recovering quickly, he started to tell the patrolmen that his identification had been lost during the canoe-dunking they had told the truck driver about—was it only two days ago? Walrus listened with seeming good humor, but it wasn't until Beth and the others joined them, supporting his story, that they relaxed, and the second cop let his hand move away from where it had been hovering disturbingly close to what Dylan assumed was a gun holster under his jacket.

Even afterward, the patrolmen—Walrus, and his partner, who looked barely a pup, probably still on his first razor—were doubtful, but polite. "They just left, after all that?" Walrus took the lead in the conversation, while the younger one wrote everything down and frowned a lot. "And you never saw any of them before?"

"The woman, yes, just like I told you. The others, never." Dylan had absolute honesty on his side, mostly. They—newly minted lovers trying to get a weekend away—had been menaced by a woman who had stalked them from Elizabeth's hometown all the way here, for no reason they could determine. They had tried to get away from her, to the point of changing their plans midtrip and ditching their luggage, but to no avail. The woman had brought goons with her to their motel room, goons with guns, and that had scared the hell out of them. They'd panicked at that point, understandably, and run. The first chance Beth got, she had called the police.

The woman had found them again at that point, and tried to force him, Dylan, into coming with them, threatening Beth unless he obeyed. However, when the news truck came by and started waving a camera around, the woman and the goons got in their car and drove away, clearly not wanting any publicity—or witnesses.

"I never even heard her name," Dylan said. "I don't even know how she learned mine!" Mostly truth, there.

Mentioning anything to do with seal-kin, magic or skin-hunters was obviously out of the question for anyone involved. Beth had emphasized—what had she called it? Right—"Keep It Simple, Stupid"—when she went over the plan the night before. The less they embellished, the more reliable they would sound. The more reliable—and stupid—they sounded, the more the cops would believe them. It was a strange theory, but it seemed to be working. The Hunter would soon learn that the media hadn't been as muzzled as well as she'd thought.

"And you never got a name, or the license plate of the car?"

"No. Sorry." He hadn't even thought to look at the car at all, once people got out of it. Beth might have, she was more used to such things, but if she had, she didn't volunteer anything. Her part in the plan at this point was to be shaken and fragile, as needed, to drive home the fact of the woman Hunter as threatening, dangerous.

"And you gentlemen can confirm all of this?" the younger cop asked the news crew. He was blond and brawny and Dylan didn't like him on sight, all the more so when his blue eyes checked Beth out, toes to ears, spending way too much time lingering on her hips and chest. The urge to head-butt the boy was repressed only because it would probably not be as effective in human form as it would as a bull seal.

"The part we saw, yes," the reporter said solemnly, and then shut his mouth with an almost audible snap. Whatever he knew, he was keeping to himself, for his own reasons. Dylan wondered, briefly, what Beth had said to him, just before the cops arrived.

"And believe me, we saw enough." The cameraman slung his equipment over his shoulder and offered his hand to the cops, who shook it automatically. "I'm Max. That's Tom, our engineer and master of the truck. Pretty boy over there's Tyler, our anchorman-in-training." The cameraman had a surprising amount of charm when he put the camera down, taking over the conversation entirely. "Man, we were totally bummed to miss a story. Not that I'm not glad you're okay, guys," he said over his shoulder to Dylan and Beth, "but man, it would totally have gotten us the lead on tonight's broadcast."

The reporter, Tyler, leaned back against the side of the van and let the cameraman roll. Beth rested against Dylan's shoulder, and he draped his arm around her, watching the younger cop open his notebook again, like he was going to start going over their story yet one more time. "I'd really like to go home now," she said in a small voice, right on cue. "It's been a horrible day."

The senior cop knocked his partner's shoulder before he could start writing anything more. The older man was well past midcareer and closing in on retirement. His partner might have wanted to push the story for more detail, but the fact that the news crew was there, and Dylan and Beth were clearly on affectionate terms—meaning that Dylan probably wasn't the "he" the 911 operator reported the caller being afraid of—supported the facts presented and smoothed over the things they weren't exactly being up front on.

"I totally understand, miss," the older man said. "Since you've chosen not to press charges, all I can do is remind you to be careful for the next few weeks, both of you, and that if you see this woman again, or any of her companions, you call us right away. Better safe than, well, you know."

"Oh, absolutely," Beth said with heartfelt agreement, widening her eyes and nodding like a little girl. Dylan was pretty sure that he heard the driver of the van stifle a snicker. They weren't buying her helpless act, either. Thankfully, the cops didn't know how strong his mate actually was.

With nothing else to do, the two cops put away their notebooks and got back into their car. After a short conversation and a call to their dispatcher, they pulled out of the parking lot, lights and sirens off this time. They passed a beat-up SUV pulling in, towing a small boat behind it.

Beth stiffened under Dylan's arm, turned to watch the newcomers. The SUV pulled off into a far corner of the lot, and a man with two young boys got out and, totally ignoring anything else going on in the parking lot, started unloading supplies for a day out on the water.

Beth shivered for real this time, unable to take her eyes off them. Dylan watched her, worried. How long was it going to take before she stopped seeing Hunters behind every stranger's face? When would she become so paranoid she would start seeing them behind a friend?

"You guys need a ride somewhere?" Tom, the van's driver, asked.

Beth forced herself to turn her back on the new-comers, responding to the offer with a smile. "We're heading to the ferry. If that's not too far out of the way for you?" She really did want to go home. Home, her own bed, her own blanket over her head, and maybe not come out for a month. Or more. Dylan could feel it in her, that longing for something familiar, something reassuring. The fact that her familiar and reassuring was so at odds with his own...

It would work out. She was his mate. It would work out. He had to believe that. He couldn't lose her, not now.

"They pay us to drive all over the place," Tyler was saying, "so one place is as good as another. If you don't mind riding in the back with the beast over there…"

Max bowed with mock gallantry and shoved open the side door. "*Mi* disaster area *es su* disaster area."

They climbed in and discovered that Max hadn't been exaggerating by much. The entire back of the van was filled with equipment, more equipment, and far too many crumpled bags from fast-food restaurants.

"They might be waiting for us," Beth said quietly, settling onto the bench seat and making room for Dylan next to her, while Max scrunched next to what looked like a generator, holding on with one hand to a bar welded to the van's side for obviously that exact holding-on purpose. "Back home."

"I know." He kept his voice low as well, although Max, sensing that they weren't in the mood for group conversation, had a pair of headphones on now, and had busied himself with some of the mysterious tech, allowing them a sense of privacy even in the crowded confines of the van. "We have cost the Hunters the profit of at least one skin, and it isn't as though my people are common on the rocks to begin with. I don't think they will try for you again, though. They're not certain enough, and we've already caused too much attention to be cast their way, just as we planned. It may be enough to make them back away permanently."

"Oh, we're not going to stop there." She sounded exhausted, but decidedly pleased with herself. "That's what I was suggesting to Tyler, when the cops showed up. He's going to sell the story. One of the tabloids, you know, those trashy newspapers that constantly proclaim Bigfoot sightings, Jesus' face seen in a sports towel, all that sort of thing."

He didn't know, actually, but it sounded fascinating.

"Nobody admits to believing the stories," Beth went on, "but a lot of people read 'em. Massive circulation. And they never let go of a story, especially one they can gore up—a couple of Photoshopped pictures of baby seals, and the suggestion of organized crime? Oh, yeah, headline material, for sure. Once tabloid reporters are on the scent of something that horrible, the Hunters won't be able to operate quite so openly as before. They might even have to hire a few lawyers to defend their people, if one of them happens to take a swing at a reporter." She was *definitely* pleased with herself.

Then she sighed, the pleasure running out of her like a stream drying up. "Let them be hunted for a while. See how much they like it."

The sound of her exhaustion cut Dylan straight to the heart, and he wanted nothing more than to make everything all better. But he had only made things worse, by changing in front of everyone like that. If that hadn't been caught on film, if nobody had seen it, they could have used the footage, gotten a media splash about crazies hunting people for a game, pressed charges, gotten the woman and her goons thrown in jail at least for a while, made even more of a tangle for the Hunters to deal with.

Max started slightly and took the headphones off, leaning into the front of the van even as the radio crackled to life, static breaking into a calm voice reeling off street names and a string of numbers that were clearly code for something major going down.

"I got it, Max. And we're on, children." Tyler leaned into the backseat area from his seat. "Guys, we're almost there, but sorry we can't stay. Job calls. Be ready to jump!"

The camera crew let them off a few blocks from the ferry station, generating not a few stares from the tourists heading out to Martha's Vineyard and Nantucket. The locals, inured to the strange attire of tourists and bred to the stoicism of true Yankees, made it their business not to notice anything was at all odd about the sight of a news van disgorging a couple into traffic and then speeding away before the sliding door was completely closed.

"Well." Dylan put his arm around her shoulders. "That was different."

"You say that like I would know what normal was."

"True." They joined the small crowd of people heading toward the dock. She leaned into his shoulder, and he felt her exhaustion again as though it was his own.

"Dylan. What you did back there, when you… changed," Beth started to say, and Dylan hung his head, anticipating her words.

"I know. I'm sorry." This was what he had been dreading, why he had put off changing, avoided every discussion of the other side of his nature. But there was no avoiding it anymore.

She stopped in the middle of the sidewalk and stared at him, moving out from under the arch of his arm. "Sorry? For what? You probably saved us—that woman wasn't the sort to back down unless her own neck was in danger. And it was…" Her voice softened as though in awe. "It was amazing to see."

Dylan hadn't realized until then exactly how much his unease about Beth's own reaction had affected him. His muscles felt as though someone had poured warm water over an icicle, making them soften and go slack in relief for the first time in days—maybe since he had woken up in that clinic and begun his pursuit.

"You weren't…disgusted?" Because there were stories told about that, too, along with the legends. The humans who had screamed, or run, or shot at them when they saw the change, who had shouted "demon" and "monster" and tried to run them off. The loved ones who turned away, when a seal-kin's secret was revealed. Elizabeth was seal-kin blood, he didn't think she would react that way…but she had been raised a human, and he hadn't *known* for certain, not until then.

"It was…" She started walking again, in sync with his steps, but she seemed to be searching for the right word. "It scared me," she admitted. "Scary—or at least, I was scared, did I mention I was scared? Because I was terrified. And it happened so fast it wasn't like I really saw anything. But no, I wasn't disgusted. It's just…"

His relief died as fast as it came. "What?"

She moved away from him, such a small movement she probably wasn't even aware of it. He was, though. Painfully. Terrifyingly. He wanted to reach for her, but was afraid to.

"Everything that's happened, what you've told me…I don't know who I am anymore. *What* I am. I think I need some time to deal with all of this. All…you. Me. What just happened." She looked down at her feet, and her next words were muffled. "Time…alone."

The relief was gone like it had never existed, replaced by the feeling of plunging into a bottomless cavern, of being pulled under a wave and knowing that he would never see the sky again. Foolishly, he had somehow thought that once he had wooed and won her, once they were safe, once she understood, she would have…

What, gone off with him? Left everything she knew behind without a second thought? Accepted the fact that she had been living a half-truth all of her life?

Yes. He really had thought that, somehow. He had really been foolish—ignorant—enough to think that he would be all that she needed.

His mother's sigh echoed in his skull. *Trust her. Even if you can't trust yourself.* Such a small, difficult thing.

"It's not… I'm not…" Beth stumbled over her words, the first time he had ever seen her uncertain, and he couldn't help himself. He put his arms around her, drawing her body close against his, feeling the way her frame shook, not from cold, or fear, but the weight of everything that had been placed on her in such a short time. And yet, even in those shivers her body rested with such trust against his, molding with such familiarity, strength to weakness, and weakness to strength, that he could not entirely despair in her hesitation.

Trust her. Was it his mother's voice? Or something deeper, sounding inside him?

He had come for a mate, and found her. He had promised not to leave her, he didn't *want* to leave her. But maybe she needed to leave him. Just for a little while…

Ignoring the crowds around them, Dylan slid his hands up her back, feeling a much more pleasant shiver travel along her spine in response, until his fingers reached the slender column of her neck and the black mass of her hair. It smelled of the horrible shampoo from the motel, and sweat and fear, and it was still a lovely, lovely smell. How could it only have been weeks since he first touched her? Surely it had been months, a year, a lifetime…

Trust.

Everything in his life had come easily, by instinct. He had trusted instinct and charm to win his mate, as though it was his right, simply by existing. That he would sweep in and carry her off.

His arrogance, his ignorance, made him want to laugh—and weep—for how easily he could have lost her. How easily he still could lose her, if he said or did the wrong thing.

Trust.

Trust that she would return. That she needed him as much as he needed her. That she would choose him, the way her great-grandfather had chosen the land.

"I love you," he said to her, the words coming, not easily, but with a sense of rightness. "I love you and I will wait for you. All you'll need to do is call me."

And then his lips were on hers, silencing whatever she might have tried to say, demanding instead a nonverbal response to his promise. There was a spark of hesitation, and then her mouth— already open to speak—relented further under the pressure of his lips, allowing him access with tongue and teeth. He nipped at her lower lip, dipping inside her mouth, tasting the particular flavor that was his Elizabeth, memorizing it, storing it so that it would remain forever in his taste buds, imprinted always in his senses.

She was flawed, imperfect, frightened, and so was he. She might be his mate, might be seal-kin blood, but there was so much between them, so much *difference,* he had no idea how they were going to make this work, *if* they could make this work.

He only knew he would be there, every step of the way, if she would only meet him equally.

He had to believe that she would.

"Get a room," someone muttered at them, and they broke apart, if only a few inches for propriety's sake.

"When you're ready," he whispered against her skin, and let go, disappearing into the crowd before she realized what he was going to do.

To an observer, it might seem as though he had merely blended with the mass of humanity swirling around them. Only Beth, listening for it, heard the gentle splash of something entering the water at the end of the pier, and swimming away.

She had a vague memory of walking from the ferry area, of finding a café and ordering a large coffee and a sandwich. She even had a vague memory of eating the sandwich, although she couldn't have said what it was, or how it tasted. All she could do was taste Dylan's lips on hers, hear the whisper of his voice in her ear.

I love you.

Others had said it to her before. She had even believed it, had believed that they believed it, taken joy in that belief, in the contact, the connection.

The words had never shattered her the way they had this time. She was numb, unable to focus, unable to comprehend anything.

He loved her. And he had left.

Just like her parents and cousin had done. There with her one moment, and gone the next. Forever.

No, stop it. It wasn't the same. It wasn't. Her parents would have come home, if they could have. They hadn't meant to die, hadn't meant to leave her all alone.

Hadn't meant to abandon her.

Dylan hadn't abandoned her, either. She was the one who had needed time.

But he didn't have to leave. Not like that.

That was what selkies did, a little voice whispered. *That's what all the legends say. They might love mortals, but they are not mortal themselves. The sea calls them home.*

"But I'm one of them, too." She said it out loud, for the first time, not caring who heard. "I'm seal-kin."

The truth of that still felt strange. How could a sane human possibly believe in that, in magic? In shape-changers? Werewolves and the like were the stuff of horror movies. Dylan, her Dylan, was nothing like that.

And yet she had seen him change, had seen—or not seen so much as sensed—his body transform from human to seal, his skin fade and stretch from one identity to the other, and yet remain, somehow, the same. She had seen the bulky, muscled bull seal, huge and glorious and terrifying, and known that it was Dylan. She would know him anywhere....

She had known him, she realized now, when he helped her escape from the Hunters that first time, swimming beside her, keeping her moving and bringing her to safety. Had known even then that the shadow in the water was nothing to be afraid of, that it—he—would protect her, aid her.

She hadn't known then that he would love her, as well.

He had come looking for a mate. A chemical

reaction, lust and a breeding frenzy… There was nothing of love in that. Nothing of choosing to be with a person, no matter the risk, no matter the cost. No matter the sacrifice.

Dylan loved her. Dylan would have died for her, to keep her safe, and considered it a fair trade.

Beth wasn't sure she believed in that sort of love. She wasn't sure she believed in selkies, in the supernatural. She was pretty sure that she didn't believe in Fate or Destiny or any of those things.

But she believed in Dylan.

Dylan of the warm brown eyes and tender embrace: the impossible innocence and sudden streaks of fierce passion. Dylan. Shape-changer. Selkie. A creature of wind and wave, not human society. Impossible. And yet there, for her. *I came for you.*

None of the labels applied. He was himself, no matter if he wore seal or human form. Not a warrior, not a fighter; he admitted that himself. But brave when it counted. Braver than she was, in so many ways. Truthful, always, even when it hurt. Loving, and protective, and…

And if he told the truth…her great-grandfather had been like him. That was what the dream-memories were telling her. Her great-grandfather had been able to change between seal and man, land and sea. Had chosen, for whatever reason, in whatever deal with the devil, to tie his children, and his children's children, to the land…and yet never be able to let go of the sea. Never, in four generations, to let go of where he had come from, what he had once been.

Not a horror movie. A love story.

Another memory came back to her, while the dregs of her coffee grew cold, and the restaurant began to empty around her. A true memory, from her own life.

Blood breeds true. Blood is thicker than water, but the water keeps it flowing. Salt in your veins, Beth. Her father used to say that, then laugh and say that he never knew what it meant, either, that it was just a family saying.

Now she knew. More, she *understood.* Or thought that she did, that she might, anyway.

So now you know, what are you gonna do about it, Miss Elizabeth? Ben's voice asked her. *It's your time. What are you gonna do?*

That, she didn't know.

Chapter 14

The waitress came by four times, pausing briefly each time by the table, before Beth shook off her emotional paralysis enough to take the hint.

"Sorry, I was just…thinking."

The waitress, a teenage girl with a long blond ponytail, looked as though she'd never thought of anything deeper than what to do that evening, but her expression and her words were both kind. "Don't you worry about it. I just go off-shift soon, and I like to get the tabs cleared before then, in case there's a problem. Sit as long as you like."

Beth smiled and handed over enough cash to pay her bill, and tucked a generous tip under the mug. She had done enough sitting. There was just one thing she had to do, before anything else.

As Beth had hoped, the town had their own library, a pretty, small, one-story brick building just off the Green, next to Town Hall, and it had evening hours. Once inside, she discovered that their inventory was heavier on children's books, DVD rentals and local tour and restaurant dining guides than anything else. It was still a library, though, and with luck it would have what she needed. Beth accosted a harried-looking volunteer, and was directed to a small back room that smelled of lemons and dust. Their mythology section was small, but unsurprisingly heavy on ocean-related topics, and there was enough material there to answer a few questions about selkies—and raise half a dozen more. She brought the books and pamphlets to the table and skimmed through them, not bothering to take notes. When she was done, she sat at the table and stared into space, slotting what she had read into the appropriate places in her mind and memory.

Selkies. Seal-kin. Shape-changers.

How much was legend based on fact and how much was complete fairy tale she didn't know, but several pieces of her own experience fit together better now.

Dylan had been right: selkies, or some similar creature, seemed to appear in every culture that had a coastline, and human/selkie love affairs were pretty much the focus of every story. Unfortunately, what she had discovered was that they were usually—at least the ones that got written about—ill-fated. The human mate was usually the one to blame, captur-

ing the selkie by dint of taking his—or more typi-
cally her—skin, and thereby trapping her on land
until she could reclaim that skin and escape. Even
the marriages that were by mutual consent hardly
ever had happy endings. Love didn't seem to con-
quer the difference between land and water.

Offspring likewise—mostly they were left without their seal-parent when she or he left, or ran off
to sea to follow as soon as they could, and were
never heard from again. Those who stayed on land,
however, grew to be charming, smooth-tongued...
and, allegedly, great fisherfolk.

Her father hadn't been able to catch a haddock
in a supermarket, from what she remembered. So
much for that myth. He had been charming, though.

And yet...these stories were myths, fairy tales.
That meant they were told and retold not merely for
entertainment, but to prove a point, or teach a
lesson. And somehow she was cynical enough to
believe that the lesson wasn't "happily ever afters
come easily." Was that all there was? Or somewhere, was there something more? How had her
great-grandfather managed to leave the sea behind,
to die an old man, on the land?

On a whim, she went into the children's section
and found and read the Hans Christian Andersen
story of *The Little Mermaid,* skimming over some
pages, lingering on others. The original story was
vastly different from the Disney version she
remembered—darker, bloodier and far more be-
lievable.

That was the moral. There was a price for everything, and the greater the request, the higher the price.

Don't ask, if you can't pay. Don't pay, if you can't live with the results.

By the time she emerged from the library, dusk had come and gone, and the town was gently lit like an old-fashioned oil painting. Still in a fog of thought and confusion, she made a phone call, got on the last outbound ferry of the evening and went home.

Joyce met her at the dock, as requested. Her old friend took one look at her face, the exhaustion and preoccupation there, and didn't ask questions about where she had been, even though she clearly wanted to. She didn't even do the usual second-best of friends in distress, and pelt her with mindless, distracting, hopefully amusing chatter. The car radio, left to a classical station, hummed gently, not enough to disturb the swirling, murky green depths of her thoughts.

It was only when they pulled up in front of her home that Joyce said anything at all. "Beth."

"Hmm?" The sound of her name barely roused her from the depths.

"Are you going to be okay?"

The wistful concern in her friend's voice demanded an answer. "Yeah. It's okay. I'm okay." But she didn't know that for certain. Didn't know anything for certain at all, right then. She leaned over the shift stick, awkwardly, and gave Joyce a hug. "Thank you," she said, and got out of the car.

Walking up the stoop and through the familiar

door of her family's house, Beth stopped and let the surroundings envelop her in the decades of history and comfort. Home. One room after another, she paced through them, letting her hand trail over the tops of bookshelves and along window ledges, touching a chair here, an antique there. Her fingers lingered over one of the hand-crafted boats, a small, perfectly reproduced square-rigger, barely the size of her palm. She picked it up and held it gently, a finger stroking along the satiny wooden sides. The care and craft that went into it, the hours spent ensuring every detail was perfect, amazed her all over again. To love something so much, and yet never go out on the real thing, never place your feet on the full-size version or feel the waves and wind rocketing you forward…where was the disconnect? How could so much love be focused on something so small? How…and why?

What was the price her great-grandfather had paid?

Without answers, Beth moved on, up the stairs and down the hallways.

She had grown up here. Her father had grown up here. Her grandfather had helped his own father build the house, adding room after room as his family grew and prospered, before it narrowed and shrunk to just her. Always looking with one eye to the shoreline, and another to the town. Never straying too far from the waters they rarely entered. Building boats they never used.

And they had been restless. Every spring, feeling the change of seasons, the pull of another world.

What she had felt wasn't strange, or sick, or weird...not by her selkie-blood, anyway. If her father had lived...he might not have been able to tell her why she felt that way, but he would have told her she wasn't alone.

She had never been alone, if only she had known.

Her feet took her, finally, inevitably, and without conscious thought, to the widow's walk.

The night sky was filled with silvery-gray clouds, threatening rain, and the air was cool and salty off the ocean. Not storm-weather, but the possibility, the potential was there. Now that she allowed herself to feel it, she couldn't avoid the knowledge.

The potential was always there. Violence in even the quietest moments. Love out of chaos, across distance.

She looked at her skin. It was pale, like Dylan's. Like her father's, and her grandfather's. It fit snugly on her flesh, covering bones and sinew and blood the way it was designed to, protecting the delicate workings inside. Shape change. Change your shape. Dylan in seal form was...he had been a seal, totally, as far as anyone could tell. But he had been Dylan, too. How did you slough it off, and become something else, and keep yourself inside? And the mechanics of it: it happened so fast, but how? How did bones change form, and what happened to the soul, the self, the human organs within? Did they change as well, become something else, or was it just the outside appearances? Did it hurt? Did it feel good?

She studied her hand, imagining it as a seal's flipper, dark brown and sleek, like a living wet suit. She visualized it that way until she *saw* the change begin, spreading from fingertip to wrist, from wrist to elbow, until it reached her shoulder, her torso…

Nothing happened. No tingle. No change. No magic.

The skin and bones remained her hand, pale pink and human. Suddenly, Dylan seemed very far away, and her blood cooled unpleasantly with a devastating sense of loss. He had been wrong. She was not seal-kin, or if she was, the blood had become too thin, the distance too great.

That was the price that had been paid.

She was landbound. He was…not. That was all there was to it.

No. Her fingers clenched on the rail, and her jaw set stubbornly in a way her friends would recognize, a determined cast to her expression that would make Jake take a step back in concern, and Ben chortle with pleasure. No, and no. Anger bubbled beneath the surface, anger and a hint of desperation. She would not accept that. He had come so far to find her, had taken such risks to be with her, had been brave enough to step back and give her time, when she knew that he would rather have gone all caveman—caveseal?— and not taken no, or even maybe, for an answer.

She would not now, after all that, merely shrug and say oh, well. She would not tamely accept failure, quietly go back to a life of good-enough and calm enjoyments, not after she had tasted the wildness of passion, of love that could be shocking and fierce and *real*. She would rather die than go back to that sort of half life.

There had to be a way to reach over the chasm between them, to teach her what to do. To discover what had brought her family here, to this spot, this place, this decision. To repay the price that had been paid, somehow.

But how? There was nobody she could ask, and neither her grandfather nor great-grandfather had been the kind to keep diaries or journals she could look to. That seemed to have been part of the price as well, to leave no trace behind in history, either human or seal-kin.

And yet... Beth stared out at the ocean, barely seeing it. She was remembering. Sharing a genetic memory, somehow. Like fixing a damaged photograph, the details were all there, just waiting to be recovered and revealed. What else did she know, that she had never known she knew?

Standing in the house her family had built, her face to the limitless ocean vista, Beth closed her eyes and tried to remember....

The sea raged, deep in its chasms, hidden by caverns of bedrock and chimneys emitting impossible steam. Ribbons of black swirled within the depths, and things with red eyes and pale flesh swam by, some fish-shaped, and some...not.

There is a price. The words rose from the depths, and echoed with hollow thunder.

You will allow us to be together? A man's voice, more solid: deep and hopeful, but cautious nonetheless. Beth knew that voice, without ever having heard it before. Her great-grandfather as a young man.

There is a price. That voice she also knew. It was cool and dark, neither masculine nor feminine but somehow both, and neither. Relentless. The endless movement of all water, the deepness and the stillness of the oceans, the restless fury of all storms, the deceptively cruel peace of dead calms. Potential, endless, recycling potential contained within it.

I will pay the price. The man again, determined, and a little desperate.

The hollow voice filled as it rose from the depth, taking on pressure, deepening and become more powerful, a storm building power. *All will pay the price,* it warned.

A vision came with the words, of generations cast up on dry shore, refused admittance to the waves, never knowing the embrace of the water or the joy of the surf. Of generation after generation down the endless line, locked within a single, human skin.

The hollow thunder became the terrifying howl of a typhoon. *There will be no return. No remission. No change for the rest of time, so long as your line continues. What was, will no longer be. For love, you must pay in love. All must pay.*

The selkie staggered under the blow. To cast off his own self, to give up forever the feel of his sealself, to never teach his children how to change, how to swim with flipper and tail, to ride the surf and sport with their kin…?

To spend the rest of his life asleep by his beloved's side. To see his children grow, every day, and watch them take mates and create laughing, green-eyed children in turn…

It was no price, what Tethys asked him to pay.

We agree. He spoke for them all, and for all of them it was done.

Beth opened her eyes, her lashes thick with salt from her tears.

"I did not agree!" she cried out into the wind. "I did not agree, Tethys!"

It was agreed. The voice was the same as in her great-grandfather's memory: cool, implacable, not unkind, but without mercy. The bargain had been struck, and could not be undone. The sea might claim her, might share her knowledge, but she was not allowed to return.

She could not change, the way Dylan did. Trying to let go of her human self, she had only felt the limitations of her body, not the promise of a greater one. She did not sense the movement of tides in her blood, only the pulse of her heart, its echoing beat moving with her, present, but too far apart.

"Call," Dylan had told her.

She couldn't. Not like this, her human body limited, her seal-kinship unfelt.

Better to be apart forever, still loving, than torn apart by this.

"And that is possibly the stupidest thing you've ever thought." Her own voice shocked her, and she gripped the railing under her fingers so tight her nail beds went white. "You're going to just give up, without a fight? Let some stupid bargain you weren't a part of determine your fate now? Is that what you survived all these years for? To give up now?"

Call.

So long as your line continues…

"My line has ended, Tethys." She didn't bother to shout this time, trusting that the sea-goddess would hear her, that her blood would carry, no matter her exile, no matter her skin-locked state. "There are no more, after me. There will be no more, not without Dylan." She knew that for truth. Without her mate, she would have no desire to create new life, no wish for children of her own.

All gone. The sea-voice sounded…surprised? Wistful. Her family might have been exiled, but they were still kin. Still Tethys's children. You never stopped loving your children.

You never truly abandoned them.

For the first time since her parents' funeral, Beth felt a pressure in her chest ease, and her vision blurred briefly with tears.

The realization emboldened her, and Beth pushed her advantage. "All gone," she echoed in agreement. "Lost, buried forever in dry land. But they never left, Tethys. Even exiled, we never went far. We never forgot the wave and the wind."

They never went back to sea. But never left it

entirely, either. Island born and island bred, surrounded forever by their lost inheritance.

The bargain was struck. Your line was cast out.

"Then why did he come to me? How did he know to find me, to love me? How did I know him, trust him, love him, and only him, of all the humans I had met in my life?"

This time, there was no answer from the goddess.

Beth lifted her tear-streaked face to the sky, where storm clouds roiled, and a lone gull circled, screaming its hunger into the wind.

Call.

Not him. Her. She understood, now.

"Tethys! Grandmother!"

The call spiraled down, not so much sinking as returning, deep into the cold waves, down beyond human endurance, well beyond selkie or seal's reach, into the beyond-depths of the ocean floor. Into the cold waters science could only guess at.

A wave rose up in the wake of that call, tsunami-huge, green and blue and black in the depths. It rose, though fast, too fast to register on any radar, and came to the surface, seeking the source of that call. Seeking her.

A terrible face formed within that rising wave, a hundred feet high and medusa-terrible, with a squid's beak set under soulless black eyes, and the mouth opened to show the jagged teeth of an ancient shark. A thousand iridescent eels writhed for hair, and gills fluttered along the barnacle-

encrusted neck. No fair mermaid, this, but a fearsome beast, a kraken, a monster of the deep. It should have been terrifying, but Beth only felt a wild exhilaration rush through her.

Tethys. Grandmother. Summoned, in truth, as can only be done by a true daughter of the sea. Beth staggered back under the vision, but did not falter. There was everything to fear…and everything to gain.

There is always a price, that terrible voice said, surrounding her, breaking around her like a storm breaking. *Even I cannot change that law. There is a price, and a price to repay the price that was paid.*

Beth spread her arms wide to the wave, and offered everything she had.

Epilogue

In the aftermath of the freak storm that rocked the Nantucket coastline, local newscasters and marine scientists scrambled for explanations and causes, while older folk and experienced sailors merely lit their candles and patted the sides of their boats, and remembered that their mistress was her own creature, neither tamed nor always explicable.

Meanwhile, the residents of Seastone picked through the debris, sorting through their belongings and taking stock of their losses. Like a sweep of God's hand, seven houses on one block were destroyed; dozens of trees on that same street downed or damaged, and three cars tossed onto their sides like abandoned toys.

Only one life was lost.

"Oh. Jesus." Jake stood at the edge of the road and stared at what had once been a lovely old home. "I knew it was bad, but..." Words failed him.

"It's like...like the house had a bull's-eye painted on it." Gena came up next to him, her hand slipping into his almost without either one of them noticing it.

"Do you think she felt anything?" He was looking for reassurance but not really listening, bending down to pick up a chunk of broken pottery.

"We don't know she was even home." But her voice wavered, and she didn't convince herself, much less him. Joyce had picked Beth up at the ferry the night of the storm, had driven her home. The battered old Toyota was one of the cars that had been damaged, and her bicycle was still chained to a splintered porch post. Unless she had walked away...

Nobody had seen her since the storm began, almost forty-eight hours ago.

"She was home. She never left. She never wanted to leave." Jake dropped the pottery and wiped his hands on his jeans. "This place was everything to her. It was...it was all she had."

He stood up and turned to look out over the road in the other direction, toward the ocean. "She loved this view." His face twisted, and he took a step forward, and then stopped. "I don't know what to do."

"You live, boy. You go on. We all go on, boy. We go on." Neither of them had noticed Glory sitting on the remains of the front steps until she spoke. "Storms come and storms go, and we mortals weather them as best we can. Neither of you were born here, it's not in your bones. Not yet. But eventually you'll understand. Or you'll go back to the mainland."

Jake turned on the old woman, glad for a target and finding comfort in his rage. "That's all you can say? Oh, well, she's dead, let's have a cuppa?"

Glory shrugged, squinting up into the bright blue sky. Her face had aged in the days since the storm hit, but there was a calmness to her that was at odds with the wrinkles. "Have a cuppa if that's what you want. Yell if you've got to. Can't hurt. Might help."

The ragged, extended yell that erupted from Jake's throat surprised them all, Jake most of all. Gena flinched, but Glory rode it out, waiting until the last raw sounds faded away, and he was left panting, his expression drained and weary.

"Feel better?" she asked him, not without compassion.

"No." But he did, somehow. The realization saddened him, rather than bringing relief, as though he had betrayed her, somehow.

Glory laughed, a harsh coughing noise. "Go home, boy. Get drunk. Remember her however you remember her. That's how we do things. Leave an old woman alone."

Jake would have argued more, just to fill the emptiness, but Gena—understanding more than she expected to—took his hand again, tugging him away down the road, speaking quietly to him.

Alone for the moment, Glory kept squinting up into the sky.

"I was thinking we'd put a monument here," she said. "For all of them, poor family. Something simple. A stone, maybe. A thing that would weather well. A thing that would remain."

"A stone would be nice," Ben agreed. Like his wife, he seemed to appear out of nowhere. "Granite. Not marble."

"No, not marble. Marble's too cold. Do you think she's happy?"

Ben sat down next to his wife on the steps, and looked up into the same patch of sky. He took her hand, holding it between both of his.

"I can't remember the last time our Beth was truly happy," he said. "Not since before the accident. But…yes. I think she's happy now. Or she will be."

Glory rested her graying head on Ben's shoulder. "Good. That's good."

Her free hand rested in her lap. The fingers unclenched, revealing a small, perfectly formed square-rigger made of mahogany, picked out of the debris. One of the masts was broken, splintered beyond repair.

Her fingers closed back around it, gently, protecting it from further harm.

Home. Her home is gone. She can feel the land at her back, a steady presence filled with people, danger, warm food and cable television. But it is at her back, now.

The past hours are blank to her. She remembers

everything before then, all that she was, all that she had not been. Then Grandmother came, the wave engulfed her, and…

A small boat floats in the water next to the rock outcrop she is perched on, the rope from its bow lying untied on the rock next to her. A small motor rested in the back of the boat, and oars were shipped along the side, allowing her to come up on her destination without alerting anyone to her presence.

She had not called the boat to her, and yet it had appeared, rising on a wave in front of her, steady as a well-trained pony as she climbed on board, dripping wet and ungainly. She had known where to point the bow of the little craft, had known when the engine died that she had enough strength to row the rest of the way to wherever it was she was going.

Here.

A hundred yards ahead of her, an unnamed island rose out of the ocean. It appeared on maps, and yet very few people ever felt the urge to visit. Those who did were greeted by the sight in front of her eyes: a narrow dock, sized for half a dozen fishing boats. One was tied up there now, with a number of figures busily doing repairs. There was no beach as such, but a handful of children played off rocks too jagged to be safe. They raced up and down the sides without fear, occasionally disappearing with a happy scream and a splash, then crawling out of the water soaking wet and laughing.

Birds soared overhead, black-tipped wings catching the morning sunlight, while other, uniden- tified birds patrolled the wet sands and rode close to the shallow waves. Fish slipped below the mirror-dark surface, while below them, an entire world went about its business.

She understood how it was done now. You didn't have to give up one skin when you put on the other; it was just there waiting, on the other side of the magic.

Not spell-magic. Heart-magic. Soul-magic. Desire-magic. What you wanted, most of all.

And with that, she slipped into the water and felt the change take place, sinew and flesh moving to accommodate her desires, until she found her seal- kin form. Not outside her, not separate, but within. Muscular and powerful, filled with joy and hunger. This...this satisfied the restlessness in her blood. But there was one more thing she needed...

Dylan, she called, knowing, instinctively, how to do so, even as she swam forward. *Dylan.*

It had been too long. What was taking so long? His restlessness had passed, leaving behind a dreary, patient weight. The others looked at him pityingly, but said nothing. There was nothing to say.

He had been sitting with his eldest aunt, telling her—once again—about Beth, about her strength and her courage, when he heard the whisper.

He didn't remember getting up, didn't know if he had made his excuses, but found himself outside, racing down from his mother's cottage, the hope he had been hoarding, a slow, steady wavelet timed to the beating of his heart, stirred again inside him.

Dylan. She called again, and the hope surged into a typhoon.

The older men doing repairs down on the beach laughed as he moved past them, but he didn't care, splashing into the water with an extraordinary lack of grace that was never part of the seal-kin's inheritance. She surged up on a rising wave, her sleek gray form changing back to mortal without hesitation, even as he caught her in his arms, bringing his tear-wet lips down on her sea-wet ones.

It was only his imagination that, even as his clean-shaven face touched hers, he felt the brush of long, textured whiskers brushing against his cheek, but his own unshaped whiskers twitched at that phantom touch.

"You called," he said, awe blending with a purely masculine satisfaction, even as the waves buffeted them, and the warmth of his body molded her flesh against his. "You called. You came."

"You were waiting," she said simply, as though there could be no other answer, and raised her face for another kiss. He touched the side of her face, as though to reassure himself that she was really there.

"What took you so long?" he asked, and then shook his head. It didn't matter. She was here. He had trusted, and she had come.

He took her up into his arms, a rough, possessive move that announced to anyone watching that she was his. His mate. *His.*

"Dylan." She laughed, shaking her head at his action, but she wasn't protesting, not really, and she let him carry her, both of them dripping wet, to the shore, to where his family—her family—was waiting.

She had come home.

* * * * *

Don't miss
HARD MAGIC
by Laura Anne Gilman
("Anna's" alter ego).
Only from LUNA Books in May 2010.

Shaw cursed and hooked his arm around Sabrina.

Despite the urgency that the deadly gunfire created, he tried to be careful with her, and he took the brunt of the fall when he pulled her to the ground. His shoulder hit hard, but he held on tight to his gun so that it wouldn't be jarred from his hand.

Shaw didn't stop there. He crawled over Sabrina, sheltering her pregnant belly with his body, and he came up ready to return fire.

This was obviously a situation he'd wanted to avoid at all cost. He didn't want his baby in the middle of a fight with these armed fugitives, but when they fired that shot, they'd left him no choice. Now, the trick was to get Sabrina safely out of there.

"Get down," someone on the SWAT team yelled from the roof of the adjacent building.

Shaw did. He dropped lower, covering Sabrina as best he could.

There was another shot, but this one came from

a rifleman on the SWAT team. Shaw didn't look up, but he heard the sound of glass being blown apart.

The shots continued, all coming from his men, which meant it might be time to try to get Sabrina to better cover. Shaw glanced at the front of the building.

So that Sabrina's pregnant belly wouldn't be smashed against the ground, Shaw eased off her and moved her to a sitting position so that her back was against the brick wall. They were close. Too close. And face-to-face.

He found himself staring right into those sea-green eyes.

How will Shaw get Sabrina out?
Follow the daring rescue and the heartbreaking
aftermath in THE BABY'S GUARDIAN
by Delores Fossen,
available May 2010 from Harlequin Intrigue.

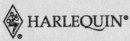

HARLEQUIN®

American ★ Romance®

LAURA MARIE ALTOM

The Baby Twins

Stephanie Olmstead has her hands full raising
her twin baby girls on her own. When she runs
into old friend Brady Flynn, she's shocked to find
herself suddenly attracted to the handsome airline
pilot! Will this flyboy be the perfect daddy—
or will he crash and burn?

Babies
&
Bachelors
USA

"LOVE, HOME & HAPPINESS"

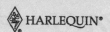

HARLEQUIN®

INTRIGUE

BESTSELLING
HARLEQUIN INTRIGUE® AUTHOR

DELORES
FOSSEN

PRESENTS AN ALL-NEW
THRILLING TRILOGY

TEXAS MATERNITY:
HOSTAGES

When masked gunmen take over the maternity ward
at a San Antonio hospital, local cops, FBI and the scared
mothers can't figure out any possible motive. Before
long, secrets are revealed, and a city that has been on
edge since the siege began learns the truth behind the
negotiations and must deal with the fallout.

LOOK FOR

THE BABY'S GUARDIAN, May
DEVASTATING DADDY, June
THE MOMMY MYSTERY, July

REQUEST YOUR
FREE BOOKS!

2 FREE NOVELS PLUS 2 FREE GIFTS!

♥ Silhouette

nocturne™

Dramatic and Sensual Tales of Paranormal Romance.

YES! Please send me 2 FREE Silhouette® Nocturne™ novels and my 2 FREE gifts (gifts are worth about $10). After receiving them, if I don't wish to receive any more books, I can return the shipping statement marked "cancel." If I don't cancel, I will receive 4 brand-new novels every other month and be billed just $4.47 per book in the U.S. or $4.99 per book in Canada. That's a saving of at least 15% off the cover price! It's quite a bargain! Shipping and handling is just 50¢ per book.* I understand that accepting the 2 free books and gifts places me under no obligation to buy anything. I can always return a shipment and cancel at any time. Even if I never buy another book from Silhouette, the two free books and gifts are mine to keep forever.

238/338 SDN E5QS

Name _____ (PLEASE PRINT) _____

Address _____ Apt. # _____

City _____ State/Prov. _____ Zip/Postal Code _____

Signature (if under 18, a parent or guardian must sign) _____

Mail to the **Silhouette Reader Service:**
IN U.S.A.: P.O. Box 1867, Buffalo, NY 14240-1867
IN CANADA: P.O. Box 609, Fort Erie, Ontario L2A 5X3

Not valid for current subscribers to Silhouette Nocturne books.

Want to try two free books from another line?
Call 1-800-873-8635 or visit www.morefreebooks.com.

* Terms and prices subject to change without notice. Prices do not include applicable taxes. N.Y. residents add applicable sales tax. Canadian residents will be charged applicable provincial taxes and GST. Offer not valid in Quebec. This offer is limited to one order per household. All orders subject to approval. Credit or debit balances in a customer's account(s) may be offset by any other outstanding balance owed by or to the customer. Please allow 4 to 6 weeks for delivery. Offer available while quantities last.

Your Privacy: Silhouette is committed to protecting your privacy. Our Privacy Policy is available online at www.eHarlequin.com or upon request from the Reader Service. From time to time we make our lists of customers available to reputable third parties who may have a product or service of interest to you. If you would prefer we not share your name and address, please check here. ☐

Help us get it right—We strive for accurate, respectful and relevant communications. To clarify or modify your communication preferences, visit us at www.ReaderService.com/consumerschoice.

SN10R